MW01128187

The Mystery Sisters
Reunion and Revenge

The Frannie Shoemaker Campground Series
Bats and Bones

The Blue Coyote

Peete and Repeat

The Lady of the Lake

To Cache a Killer

A Campy Christmas

The Space Invader

Real Actors, Not People

We Are NOT Buying a Camper! (prequel)

Also by Karen Musser Nortman
The Time Travel Trailer

Trailer on the Fly

Trailer, Get Your Kicks!

Happy Camper Tips and Recipes

Foliage

and

Fatality

The Mystery Sisters Book 2

by Karen Musser Nortman

Cover Art by Ace Book Covers

Copyright © 2018 by Karen Musser Nortman. All rights reserved. No part of this book may be reproduced in any form by any electronic or mechanical means (including photocopying, recording or information storage and retrieval) without permission in writing from the author.

This is a work of fiction. Names, characters, places and incidents are either the product of the author's imagination, or are used fictitiously, and any resemblance to actual persons, living or dead, business establishments, events, or locales is purely coincidental.

TABLE OF CONTENTS

CHAPTER ONE

LIL

MAX'S RED STUDEBAKER STARLIGHT coupe hugged a curve as the narrow road turned and dropped down a steep hill. In the passenger seat, her sister, Lil Garrett, sucked in her breath and gripped the road atlas spread open on her lap.

Max pointed at the dash. "I don't know why you are bothering with that atlas. Why don't you just use the GPS?"

Lil shut her eyes for a second. "I just like atlases. And I like the big picture."

Max snorted. "What a waste of time."

"Like I'm really busy."

"You're missing the scenery."

The Pennsylvania highway wound through overhanging trees draped with crimson and gold leaves. Occasionally an oak that hadn't turned yet or a bare ash broke up the kaleidoscope of color, just enough to emphasize the vibrant hues.

"No, I'm not. It's beautiful. I'm so glad we decided to take this trip in the fall. I never realized Pennsylvania was so wooded."

KAREN MUSSER NORTMAN

"Didn't you pay attention in school? The name means 'Penn's Woods.'"

"School was sixty years ago. Don't be so crabby."

"Then don't be so dense."

Rosie, Max's large Irish setter, sat in the back seat with her head resting on the front seat between the two sisters. She rolled her eyes back and forth as she followed the conversation, or at least the sounds of their voices. .

NEITHER SISTER SPOKE AGAIN until they arrived at a crossroads with a large fuel plaza and truck stop. Max pulled up to a pump and turned off the car.

"This will be our last stop until we get to Terry's."

Lil opened her door. "Fine." She stalked into the convenience store. After using the restroom, refreshing her makeup and fluffing her latest haircut, she returned to the store and browsed a snack counter. She bagged two pork egg rolls off a warming rack and was looking for the fountain drinks when Max came up behind her.

"Are you about ready? We'll never get there at this rate."

Lil seethed but held back her anger. "Be right there. Do you want anything?"

"No." Max eyed the egg rolls. "You going to eat those in my car?"

"I'll be careful, I promise."

"Even if you don't spill, the whole car will smell like garlic and soy sauce."

Lil didn't reply—she couldn't and remain civil. She took her purchases to the cash register. Every trip she and Max took, and that was at least three or four times a year, they reached this point of dissension before they reached their destination.

One would think that two women in their seventies would be able to maintain a cordial atmosphere, but it seemed the sibling rivalry was just too strong. She paid for her snacks and straightened her brown and gold cardigan, decorated with fall leaves in duplicate stitch, as she followed her sister back to the car in silence.

Max had let Rosie out, walked her along the edge of the parking lot, and given her a little water. The dog now awaited their return with her head hanging out the window.

Determined to improve the atmosphere, Lil cheerfully said as they pulled out of the truck stop, "It looks like we have about sixty miles left."

"Fifty-seven, actually."

"Okay."

Lil nibbled at her egg rolls, careful not to get any drips on the pristine interior of the classic car or her own carefully chosen outfit. She wiped her fingers and tucked the used napkin and wrappings into a side pocket of her tote where she kept a Ziploc bag just for such trash.

She turned and watched out the window. They were headed for Burnsville, where her son Terry had moved eight months earlier with his wife Melody and children.

Terry had taken a job as a loan officer at a local bank, and this was Lil's first visit to their new home.

Max and Lil, in an earlier, more congenial, conversation, decided that the fall would be a perfect time to visit Pennsylvania. Based on the scenery, they certainly had made a good decision. If they didn't kill each other before they got to Terry's.

TERRY AND MELODY GARRETT lived in a white, traditional, two-story colonial with green shutters on a wide street lined with oaks and maples. Neat shrubs interspersed with cushion mums in gold, purple, and rust surrounded the house.

"What a beautiful place!" Lil said as they pulled in the driveway.

"It is nice," Max agreed in a grudging tone. She rolled down her window to get the food smells out of the car while she unloaded the luggage.

The front door of the house opened and a whirling dervish with red Orphan Annie curls exploded down the steps. "Granny Lil!" shouted the dervish as she ran into Lil's arms.

"Ren! I can't believe how you've grown." Lil kissed the little girl on the cheek. She and Max had had a lengthy discussion in the car about Ren's name. Max: "What the hell kind of name is *Ren* anyway?" Lil: "It's short for Rendall." Max: "What the hell kind of name is *Rendall* anyway?" And so on.

But regardless of what Max thought of the name, Ren was a beauty, and one of those children interested in everything. At six years old, she loved toads, took tap dancing lessons, and planned to be an Olympic gymnast. However, she told Lil on the phone that she didn't need to take gymnastics lessons. She already knew how to do a cartwheel.

Now she hugged Rosie and allowed the huge dog to lick her face, giggling at the sensation. Then she grabbed Lil's hand and tugged her toward the house. "Come and see my new turtle! And Rival got in trouble for tearing a hole in his closet ceiling!"

Lil held back. "What? Wait—you can show and tell me everything later. I need to help Aunt Max with our suitcases." She walked back behind the car for her roll-behind suitcase and matching tote.

A deep voice boomed behind Lil. "I'll get those, Mom."

She turned and looked up at her handsome, now middle-aged son. He was a little thicker through the middle and thinner on top, but his eyes had the same ornery twinkle.

"Terry! So great to be here." She almost teared up.

He laughed. "It's about time. Aunt Max, how are you?"

Max hefted the strap of her old duffel bag over her shoulder. "Fine, Terry. Glad to have arrived." She gave Lil a sideways glance.

"I'll take that, too." He moved the duffel to his own shoulder, and pulling Lil's suitcase behind, started up the sidewalk. "Follow me."

His wife, Melody, held the door for them. "Welcome! The kids have been beside themselves all day. They have so much to tell you."

"Ren already informed me." Lil laughed and then caught sight of the wide and long staircase leading up from the entry. Her dismay must have shown on her face because Terry said, "Don't worry, Mom. You chicks have a room on this floor. But I'm afraid the kids will drag you upstairs sometime for their show-and-tell."

Max raised her eyebrows. "Chicks?"

Lil tapped her on the arm. "We need to take compliments where we can get them. Lead on, Terry."

He headed through a wide door on the right of the hall into a living room that stretched from the front to the back of the house. A large brick fireplace with a white mantle centered the opposite wall flanked by bookcases. Transom windows above the bookcases, as well as tall windows in the front and French doors in the back, let plenty of daylight into the room. Terry led them to a door in the far back corner at the end of the bookcases.

As he flung open the door, he said, "I hope you don't mind sharing quarters."

Lil had expected this, but Max looked a little surprised at the suggestion. Noticing her expression, Terry added, "If not, we do have extra rooms upstairs, but we thought you'd both prefer to be down here."

Ren danced and whirled around the room, nearly knocking Max over. Max caught herself, surveyed the room, and gave him a bright smile. "This will be fine." She pointed at the twin Jenny Lind beds on the far wall. "Those are Grandma Bruns' beds and the Trip Around the World quilts, if I'm not mistaken."

"They are," Terry said. "Mom passed them on to us."

Ren stopped and looked at the beds. "Who is Grandma Bruns?"

Lil pointed at herself and Max. "Our grandmother. Your dad's great-grandmother. Your great-great-grandmother. She made those quilts—they must be over a hundred years old."

"Wow." Ren skipped over and ran her hand reverently over one of the coverlets, tracing the rows as she talked. "She must have been really *great*. I like these because the little squares are *very* light blue in the center and then around the outside they get darker and darker and darker..."

"Okay, we get it." Her dad laughed. "Would you like to show Granny Lil and Aunt Max the bathroom and the closet and how the TV works?"

"Sure!" She grabbed Lil's hand.

"When you're done, come out on the porch. Melody has some spiced cider and gingersnaps for you."

"Thank you, Terry," Max said. "This is really wonderful." After her sister's surliness earlier, Lil was relieved at her apparent change of heart.

Ren led them to the en suite bath complete with a blue and white tiled walk-in shower, and slid open the closet doors with a flourish. She showed them the sitting area and the remote for the TV.

"And these doors go out to the back yard and our swings, and those go to the scream porch."

Max raised her eyebrows. "*Scream* porch?"

Ren nodded. "Yeah, they call it that because it's all covered with scream. It keeps the bugs out."

"I see. That's good to know. You want to take us there for cider and cookies?"

"Okay!"

Rosie had done her own reconnoiter of the room and, apparently satisfied, waited eagerly by the doors. Max pulled an old blanket out of a tote to keep her off the furniture.

The second set of French doors, as pointed out by Ren, led onto the wide porch that extended across the back of the house from the guest suite to another wing, also accessed with French doors.

"That's my mom and dad's bedroom."

"How nice," Lil said. "That way your mom doesn't have to go up steps."

Ren pulled a chair away from a round stone-topped table and plopped down in it. "She doesn't have to anyway. There's an elevator in the lawn-dree room. I'll give you a ride later." Max chuckled at the girl's seriousness and pronunciations.

Melody Garrett had been diagnosed with multiple sclerosis about five years earlier, which limited some of her activity. Lil never ceased to be amazed, though, at the way that she coped.

"Where's your brother?" Lil asked.

Ren lowered her voice to a whisper. "He's doing something speshal up in his room. It's a surprise for you."

"Okay, then."

Lil took the moment to check out the rest of the porch. Beside the doors from the bedroom wings, two other sets of French doors gave access from the living room and apparently the kitchen. The flagstone floor and the beamed ceiling gave a rustic feel, accented by the patio furniture in natural colors.

Terry and Melody came out bearing a tray of glasses, a pitcher and a plate of cookies. They had each gotten their cider and a cookie, when another whirling dervish came through the living room doors. This time it was red-headed, freckled Rival, two years older than his sister and every bit as exuberant. He carried a package wrapped in construction paper, secured by what appeared to be several rolls of cellophane tape. Lil hoped Max didn't feel compelled to comment on what the hell kind of name Rival was.

CHAPTER TWO

LIL

RIVAL SLAPPED THE PACKAGE on the table in front of Lil, nearly upsetting her cider.

"This is for you, Granny Lil!"

Lil hugged him. "Thank you!" Before she opened the package, she sat back and looked him up and down. "You have gotten so tall. How do you like your new house?"

"It's cool. Open your present."

"Okay, okay. Did you make this?" She carefully pulled at the ends, trying not to tear the paper. Who knew what work of art she might ruin if she did? Inside, was a handmade booklet held together with staples and paper clips. The cover, orange construction paper, displayed the title *Halloween*, enhanced with stickers of ghosts, pumpkins, and witch hats.

"It's a book, and I made it myself, and it's about Halloween!"

"We never would have guessed," Max said drily, earning a frown from her sister.

Rival appeared oblivious to any undercurrents. "And guess what? My dad works for the bank, and they have a haunted house, and he's *in charge* of it this year!" He took a breath.

"How exciting!" Lil looked at Terry. "I hope the bank isn't haunted?"

Terry grinned. "Not that we know of. The haunted house is a fund raiser for a new school auditorium. Several community groups will help staff it. It opens tomorrow, as a matter of fact."

Melody said, "It has taken all of his spare time for the last several weeks. It's pretty spectacular."

"We should take them over to see it today!" Rival said.

Ren, who had been coloring, looked up. "Yeah, Dad, can we?"

"I guess we could." He winked at Lil. "Not every mother has a son with a key to a haunted house. But it will really be better with the people playing the parts once it opens."

"Some of the stuff goes by itself, though," Ren said. "We helped put up cobwebs."

Max laughed. "When your grandma and I were kids, we always had to take the cobwebs down."

Ren frowned. "Take them down? Why?"

"Our mother didn't like cobwebs."

"That's weird," Ren said.

In the end, they decided to check out the haunted house before supper. Max put Rosie in their room with her blanket. She flopped down, rested her head on her paws, and sighed. She gazed up at Max with sad, brown eyes.

11

ON THE DRIVE to the haunted house, Terry explained its origins. "It's known as the Kell house. The last owner died several years ago, but had been in a nursing home for a long time so the house really fell into disrepair. The bank is the executor of the estate but hasn't been able to sell the house. This fall we got the idea to use it as a haunted house for a fundraiser."

He turned off the main road and headed out of town. The house, a large Victorian bereft of paint, stood at the end of a lane overhung with trees. Hand-painted signs along the lane denoting hours of operation and sponsors did not offset the natural spookiness of the setting. However once they passed the signs and reached the front porch, the isolation descended.

Lil felt an almost physical sense of gloom. She shuddered and then smiled down at her grandchildren. "It *is* spooky!"

"Just wait 'til you get inside." Rival insisted. He jiggled up and down as his dad fiddled with the door key. Finally, Terry used a shoulder against the side of the door and it inched open, protesting loudly.

Lil peered around him into the entry hall, and Max crowded behind her. Even though it was still daylight, the trees around the house and the lack of windows in the entry hall cast a twilight dimness over everything.

Terry pushed a switch, and a bare bulb suspended from the ceiling created a harsh glare. An open staircase to their right led up and disappeared into a dark hallway.

Pocket doors on the left were closed, as was a single door straight ahead.

"There'll be a lovely witch here to welcome victims — I mean, guests." Terry rubbed his hands together and cackled.

Ren pulled on Lil's hand and motioned her to bend down. "The witch is my mommy," Ren whispered.

"Oh, my! She *will* be a lovely witch."

Melody looked embarrassed, but smiled at Ren. "Don't give away all of the secrets."

Rival pointed up at a mass of white fuzz in the corner of the staircase. "I put that cobweb up."

"You did a good job. But we need to pull it apart a little more. It's too bunched up," Terry said. "Let's check out the living room." He pulled the pocket door open.

Amorphous shapes shrouded in sheets appeared in the gloom. Terry pressed a button on a device hidden on a shelf. Blue lights near the floor tucked behind furniture added an eerie glow to the room, casting elongated shadows on the walls. Mist or smoke wafted from the fireplace and an ugly chandelier swayed slightly creating an occasional brassy tinkle. More cobwebs hung from the beams.

As her eyes became accustomed to the dim light, Lil picked out a person — no, not a real person — standing behind a draped wingback chair. Claw-like fingers rested on the wings and a leering face leaned over the back, inviting her to sit.

Rival noticed the expression on her face. "Scared you, didn't it, Grandma?" He had a satisfied smirk on his face.

"It certainly did!"

Max laughed. "She always was a scaredy-cat." But she jumped when the lid on a wooden box on an end table beside her creaked open, and a gray hand emerged.

Terry smiled at his mother, waggling the remote along his side where Max couldn't see it.

The dining room, separated from the living room with an archway and oak pillars, held a long table with a variety of Adams family-styled dummies propped in the chairs. Zombie-type faces with stark make-up leered at one another across the table. A chandelier matching the one in the living room dripped cobwebs over the table. Formal china and crystal completed the setting.

"Is that our mother's soup tureen?" Max pointed at a large Haviland footed tureen with gold trim.

Terry grimaced. "Um, yeah. But we will have volunteers in every room making sure nothing gets touched."

"I certainly hope so. That is quite valuable."

"Oh, Max," Lil said. "It'll be fine. *You* never wanted any of her china."

"That doesn't mean I thought it should be treated carelessly."

Melody held up her hands. "Aunt Max, we can certainly replace it. We didn't mean to offend. We'll take it home with us and pick up something at the local thrift shop."

Max waved her hand. "Don't worry about it. I guess it's not my decision to make."

"I guess not," Lil muttered.

"No, I'm sorry," Terry insisted. "I wasn't thinking. We'll take it when we leave."

Rival and Ren watched this exchange with some impatience, hopping up and down and trying to pinch each other.

"The kitchen! The kitchen!" Ren insisted, as she led the way through a swinging door. It emitted appropriate creaks.

Gray light from the cloud-obscured sun and more windows made the kitchen slightly brighter than the other rooms.

Max pointed at a menu taped to the wall. In block letters, it said 'Finger Foods', 'Arm Roast', 'Liver', and 'Blood Pudding'. "Very clever," she said.

On the counter lay a butcher knife dripping with 'blood' and part of a leg—plastic, Lil hoped. Bones of various sizes were piled on a platter on the kitchen table.

At the old cookstove, a skeleton, suspended with fishing line and dressed in a bright, red-checked apron tied around its bony middle, grinned garishly as she (he?) waved a spatula over a skillet. Just the air currents in the room were apparently enough to provide the life-like movement.

Melody pointed out a huge hairy spider on the ceiling. "I know it isn't real, but that thing gives me the creeps every time."

15

Rival took Lil's hand and pulled her back toward the entry hall. "The best stuff is upstairs. Wait 'till you see the playroom."

They tromped up the wooden steps with Terry in the lead, so that he could turn on the lights.

Several closed doors led off a long hallway at the top. Large black and white photographs of stern Victorians with stiff collars and rigid hairdos hung on the walls in ornate frames.

Terry opened the first door on the left. A sparse bedroom held only an iron bed, a tall dresser, and a wooden chair. The faded quilt on the bed provided little color, and light from the windows was filtered through dusty brown shades.

Lashed to the chair was a dummy of a woman dressed in a high-necked, long white dress, her mouth contorted in a silent scream. Blood dripped down her face, the result of a small axe buried in the top of her head.

"Oh, ick!" Lil covered her mouth. "She looks so life-like!'

"For a dead person," Max added.

"She's pretty gruesome," Terry agreed. "The woman who did all of the manikins is a window dresser over in Pittsburgh. She did a great job, but some of them are a little over the top."

Melody said, "I think it's a bit much for children."

"Maybe I should have her tone it down," Terry said.

"Even if you just removed the axe..." Lil suggested.

16

Terry nodded. "I think you're right. Let's move on."

In the bathroom, a witch stirred an empty claw-footed tub with a long paddle. "We'll put dry ice in there for the public showings," Terry said.

An open casket on a stand was the only thing in the next room. Terry pushed a button on a remote by the door, and a vampire-like creature sat up, turned his head, and said 'good evening' in a voice from the grave.

Rival doubled over. "I *love* that!"

Max laughed at the boy's expression. Lil felt the tension between her family and Max was somewhat eased.

Terry smiled. "But next is Rival's favorite: the playroom."

"Make Grandma and Aunt Max go in first!" Rival shouted.

Lil stopped and looked at Terry. "This sounds suspicious."

"It is." He opened the next door and, with a sweeping gesture, ushered them into the room.

Max stepped in first, determined not to be frightened by a haunted house for children. Lil followed right behind her.

A large box, four or five feet tall and painted in a red and yellow diamond pattern, stood to the left of the door. The two women examined it, and Max said to her sister, "It reminds me of —" just as the top slammed open and a grotesque figure popped up swaying on springs and leering down at them. A pointed hat with bells, a long

17

sharp nose, a ruff around the neck, and a striped costume completed the picture.

Lil put her hand on her heart. "A Jack-in-the-Box?"

Max gasped. "Yes, I think that's it."

Lil looked at Ren and Rival. "What are you guys trying to do to your grandma?"

They giggled and hid behind their dad.

"So what else do you have to show us in this room?" Max asked sternly, but then grinned at the kids.

Terry wielded his remote again, and the lights dimmed while a line of jack o'lanterns with malicious grins appeared along the far wall. Discordant music came out of overhead speakers and some kind of glowing projectiles flew across the room in front of them.

Max and Lil jumped back toward the doorway. "What is *that*?" Lil yelled.

Terry softened the music. "Tennis balls with glow-in-the dark paint. One of those machines that pitches them for dogs."

"Good thing Rosie isn't here," Max said.

Terry turned the lights back up and the music off. The tennis balls stopped hurtling but continued to bounce around the room. Ren and Rival rushed to pick them up and return them to the ball launcher.

"Had enough, ladies?" Terry asked. "The big opening is tomorrow and there'll be a lot more to see then."

"It's really great, Terry," Lil said. "It should be a huge success. Do you need any more volunteers?"

He looked surprised. "Sure! You want to do that?"

"I'd love to," Lil said.

Max nodded. "Me too. Sounds like fun."

"Great! Maybe we'll start you out taking tickets and filling in, but Monday we have a bus tour coming through. One of those fall leaf tours. Some of our volunteers are not retirees and have to be back at work then. We could use more help."

Melody motioned to the kids. "Did you get everything picked up?"

"Yes!" they chorused, accompanied by a couple of fist bumps.

They were so loud going down the wooden steps that Terry called "Quiet down! You'll wake the dead."

That got them giggling. and they tiptoed the rest of the way with exaggerated steps. When they got to the entrance hall, Terry said, "I'll grab that soup tureen and we'll find something else tomorrow."

Maxine grabbed his arm and smiled at him. "Forget it, Terry. And that I snapped at you about it. I apologize. This is probably the best use it could get."

"You're sure?"

"I'm sure."

ON THE RETURN HOME in Terry's SUV, the kids peppered Max and Lil with questions about their favorite parts of the haunted house and where they were most scared. Their excitement carried through supper and all the way to bed.

Chapter Three

Max

THE NEXT MORNING, Maxine woke from a pleasant night's sleep. She enjoyed a hot shower and dressed for the day. The sun began to make streaks across the back lawn.

The first order of the day was to take Rosie out for her morning walk. The sidewalk followed the winding street down to a bridge over a rocky creek. Max let Rosie off her leash and stood on the bridge leaning over the stone railing to watch the dog frolic in the water. After a few minutes, she called the dog, and they continued around the neighborhood. The gracious lawns, old trees decked with fall color, and the crisp blue sky combined to give her a feeling of complete peace.

Back at the house, she dried Rosie off with an old towel that she kept in her car and led her back through the house. Melody told her the night before that the coffee was on a timer and the newspaper would be at the front door before dawn. She found the newspaper under a bush and helped herself to the coffee.

Soon she was ensconced on a chaise lounge on the 'scream' porch with her coffee and the paper, watching the early birds at the feeder outside. Rosie appeared exhausted by her swim and didn't even feign interest in the wildlife.

Max had to admit that Terry and Melody had picked a great spot for a house. The back yard was surrounded by trees and shrubs, now dressed in their fall colors. Behind them, rounded hills displayed more color.

Burnsville was nestled in the hills of western Pennsylvania — one of those villages being revitalized by attracting day tourists to antique shops, boutiques, small museums, and specialty cafes. The haunted house should fit right in with that clientele. Max looked forward to helping with the project.

She had been worried that this visit would be on the dull side. She and Lil traveled together several times a year, and of course Lil wanted to visit her son and family. Max thought the entire time would be spent sitting around while Terry and Melody droned on about their children's clever sayings and accomplishments.

Not only was that not the case, but Max was enjoying that cleverness first hand. She had never had children and didn't normally seek out their company. Her teaching career had been spent with college students and that was young enough for her. But Ren and Rival — despite their odd-as-heck names — since she had last seen them a few years earlier, had developed such an unaffected and refreshing view of the world that she found them quite funny.

She had dozed off when the slam of one of the French doors brought her full awake.

"Whoops." Ren stood there looking at her with one small hand covering her mouth. "I dint know you were asleep."

Max straightened her gray sweater. "I was just dozing. How are you this morning?"

"Great!" Ren said. "After school, the haunted house is going to open."

"That will be exciting," Max agreed. "I love your outfit."

The little girl wore a baggy turquoise sweater, a short ruffled red skirt, black and white striped leggings, and ankle high red boots. She twirled, holding her arms up. "I picked it out myself."

"You have excellent taste."

"I know," Ren said.

Max glanced at her watch. "What time do you have to go to school?"

"Eight-fifteen."

"Do you need help with your hair?"

Ren's red curls stuck out on one side and were flat on the other. The little girl put one hand up to her head and grinned. "I forgot. Be right back!" She twirled again and rushed back into the house. Lil and Melody soon joined Max on the porch, and they chatted until Ren and Rival came out balancing bowls of cereal and glasses of orange juice.

Ren noticed Max watching her progress to the table. "Mom lets us fix our own breakfast."

Melody looked a little embarrassed. "Terry and I feel it's good for them to take on whatever responsibilities they can handle. Some call it free-range parenting, like it's a bad thing."

"I think it's great," Max said.

Terry walked in, tightening his tie. "I have to go in to work this morning. Mel thought maybe you would like a little tour of downtown?"

"Sounds good," Lil said. "Is there anything we can do to help get ready for the haunted house opening?"

"No, I think we're in pretty good shape. But we'll give you jobs tonight." He leaned over and kissed Melody. "I'll see you all later."

After he left, Melody said to the kids, "Finish up your breakfasts. It's about time to take you to school."

"Can I do that?" Max asked.

Rival dropped his spoon in his bowl. "In your car?"

Max nodded.

"Cool! Can she, Mom?"

Melody smiled. "Of course. You have to behave."

"We will! We will!" Ren shouted and returned to her bowl of cereal with gusto. They finished their breakfasts in record time and gathered their backpacks. Max was glad they would be strapped in with seat belts.

Lil rode along and helped Max field the kids' constant questions. By the time they unloaded them at the school and got back in the car, Max laughed. "I'm exhausted!"

23

Lil agreed. "I need a nap. I don't know how Melody does it."

Max pulled away from the school curb. "She seems to cope very well."

"She does."

THEY FOUND MELODY relaxing on the porch with the morning paper. She looked up, smiled, and started to get up.

"Stay still," Lil said. "Can I get you anything?"

"No. I was just enjoying the quiet. Those two can sure fill up a space with noise. But I thought you wanted to go downtown?"

Max waved a hand. "Later. Absolutely no rush. I could do some reading myself."

Lil offered to help with laundry or vacuuming but Melody refused. "We all work on laundry and Terry insists on having a cleaning service once a week." She winked at them. "He doesn't know that I do some touching up in between, and don't you dare tell him. I need *some* activity."

Max looked at her watch. "How about if we go downtown about 10:00?"

"Sounds good to me," Melody said. "Lil?"

"Great."

THEIR FIRST STOP was the bank. Terry spotted them from inside a glass cubicle where he was standing and talking to an elderly couple. They apparently were finished as they shook hands, and he held the door for them.

"Welcome! How about a tour of our massive financial facility?" He grinned as he swept his hand around the fairly new, although moderately-sized, room. Two granite-topped counters stood in the center with slots for pens and envelopes. A counter with three teller windows stood on one side with a row of glass-fronted offices like Terry's on the other. A larger office with fewer windows was in the back.

"Of course," Lil said.

"I'll just wait in your office," Melody said.

Terry pointed at the big office in the back. "First, I want you to meet our president." He led them back, tapped on the door and opened it a crack. "Camille? Have you got a minute? There're some people here I would like you to meet."

A petite, striking woman with dark upswept hair got up and came around her desk, hand outstretched. Her broad smile was welcoming and extended to her eyes. A beautiful fall scarf artfully arranged around her neck complemented her rust colored suit.

"This is my mother, Lillian Garrett, and my aunt, Maxine Berra. My boss, Camille Bamford."

The women shook hands.

Camille Bamford said, "Terry has told me so much about you. You're the two women who travel all over together? It sounds so great—makes me wish I had a sister."

Max and Lil gave each other sideways glances and grinned. "It is great—most of the time," Lil said.

Camille raised her eyebrows but didn't question the comment. "I can't tell you how much I have enjoyed working with your son. He's turned out to be a great hire for us."

"Thank you. He seems to be very happy here."

"Should I leave?" Terry asked. "I mean, if you want to talk about me?"

Lil looked up at him and patted him on the arm. "No, dear. We've pretty much exhausted that subject."

Camille laughed. "I see where you get your sense of humor." She glanced at her watch. "I have a short meeting with some of the board members, and then Art's coming to take me to lunch at the City Center. Why don't you all join us? I'd love to hear more about your trips."

"That would be great," Terry said. "I'm going to give them a tour of the rest of the bank and a couple of shops, so why don't we meet you there?"

"About noon?"

"Works for us."

After a brief trip around the bank and meeting the rest of Terry's co-workers, they collected Melody from Terry's office and headed down the street toward the cafe. Max and Lil stopped in a couple of the shops along the way, so that it was almost noon by the time they reached the City Center Cafe, which faced an open plaza with a small fountain surrounded by benches.

"City Center is an ambitious name for a spot in a town like Burnsville, but it's very popular," Terry said. "Would you like to eat inside or out?"

"It's such a beautiful day," Max said. "I vote for outside."

"Me, too," Lil said.

They chose a table near the door, under the shade of a large, striped awning. A waiter brought menus and took their drink orders.

"So who is Art? Camille's husband?" Max asked.

Terry smiled. "I think he'd like to be. No, just a significant other. Art Carnel. Camille is not only very attractive and an excellent boss, but she is the heir to the Bamford fortune—goes back to the shipping and railroad barons more than a century ago. And she's very generous with it as well."

Max leaned over and said in a low voice, "Are you saying this Art is a gold digger?"

"Later," Terry said. "Here they come."

Max looked up with surprise at the approaching couple. She had expected Art to be tall and distinguished, sort of a Cary Grant type. Instead, the man who held Camille Bamford's arm was not much taller than she and on the rumpled side of bandbox grooming. His salt-and-pepper hair was parted on the side but other than that went its own way. His eyes crinkled as he made some comment that brought a burst of laughter from Camille.

Terry jumped up and pulled out a chair for his boss. As she sat, he leaned past her and shook hands with Art. He then made introductions.

Camille and Art picked up their menus and opened them briefly. Camille closed hers and smiled. "I always order the same thing. Love their Cobb salad."

Art waved the waiter over. "I think we're ready to order." Then he realized he didn't know about the others. "Are we?" He glanced around the group.

They all nodded.

When the waiter left, Camille looked at Lil and Max and said, "Now. I want to hear all about these trips. Do you always drive?"

Max picked up her spoon and twirled it. "Yes. We like to be mobile when we get to our destination."

Terry jumped in. "Wait until you see Aunt Max's car. A red 1950 Studebaker—" He looked at Max questioningly.

"Starlight coupe," she finished.

Camille leaned back in her chair. "Wow! So where do you go?"

"I live in Colorado and Lil lives in Kansas," Max said. "We try and go West at least once a year and one Eastern trip."

"Last year, we came through this area on our way to Mystic, Connecticut, but Terry hadn't move here yet. Then in the fall, we went down to Santa Fe and over to California," Lil added.

They each told about several of their adventures, ending with a trip the previous summer to a family reunion in Minnesota. "And Max helped solve a murder while we were there," Lil said.

Art raised an eyebrow. "Really? A murder?"

"It wasn't just me," Max said. "Lil helped."

Camille moved her arms off the table as the waiter delivered their plates. "That's amazing. Terry, did you inherit any of this sleuthing ability?"

Terry put his hands up. "Not me. That is, not any more than it takes to sniff out a deadbeat looking for a loan."

They laughed and Max said, "That's enough about us —probably too much. Mr. Carnel, what do you do? Or are you retired?"

"Semi-retired. I dabble in investments. I will consider myself successful if I ever get Camille to let go of some of her money."

Laughter again, but Max thought it was an odd thing to say, and certainly fraught with double meaning. The discussion turned to the haunted house project.

"Lil and Max have volunteered to help out," Melody said. "Especially for the bus tour on Monday."

Camille clapped her hands. "That's wonderful! I've been worried that we wouldn't have enough helpers for weekdays, and that's when most of the bus tours come through."

Lil nodded. "It's a pretty amazing project. Terry took us through yesterday and he said there'll be more going on when it actually opens."

"We have a number of 'actors'" —Camille used air quotes— "who will add more spice. Did you get to see the garden?"

Terry shook his head. "I think they need to see that at night. We went during the afternoon."

"You're right. Art will be reading ghost stories in the garden too."

Art gave an eerie cackle.

"I'm convinced," Max said.

They finished their lunches and walked back toward the bank where Melody had left her small SUV. It was too difficult for her to get in and out of Max's car, but Max promised Camille she would bring it down sometime during the visit.

When they were back in the car, Melody said, "Would you like to stop any where else, or do you want to go back and rest up for tonight?"

Max suspected it was Melody who needed the rest, so she said, "I'm ready for a nap. It will be a busy night."

CHAPTER FOUR

LIL

A COUPLE OF HOURS rest in the quiet house turned out to be a good thing. When the children came home from school, their excitement over the opening of the haunted house filled the house with noise. Terry grilled some burgers for supper and Lil fixed some hash browns and green beans. Melody would be driving herself after she got in her costume, so the rest piled in Terry's car about an hour before the opening.

When they arrived, Terry put the kids to work cutting up slips of paper for a raffle. A drawing the last night of the haunted house would split the take between the winner and the auditorium fund. Lil and Max set up folding tables on the porch to collect admission, the job Terry had assigned them for the night.

Art Carnel arrived shortly, dressed in a vampire costume. His hair was covered in white powder and stuck up every direction. He carried a book of scary stories for kids.

Terry welcomed him and said, "Art, would you show Mom and Aunt Max the garden? They haven't seen it yet."

Art bowed and said in a sepulchral voice, "Certainly, Ladies. Right this way." He led them through the house to the kitchen. A back door led to a small enclosed porch. They could see amorphous shapes through the porch windows. Art flipped a couple of switches and led them outside.

"Ohhh!" Lil said. "This is beautiful."

In the dark, pots of white petunias and mums along a mulch-covered path glowed in special lighting. Shrubs and trees—some bare and some with rusty leaves—were spotlit from below emphasizing their skeletal shapes. But most eye catching were the graceful and ethereal figures of women in ball gowns that glowed white and swayed in the slight breeze.

"How did they do that?" Max asked, pointing at the figures.

Art rubbed his hands together, grinning. He seemed to genuinely enjoy playing his part. "Chicken wire sprayed with glow-in-the dark paint. Then they're suspended from the branches with fishing line. Aren't they marvelous? The high school art class made them."

Max and Lil followed him through the garden, stopping to examine ghouls and monsters around every turn and exposed with dramatic lighting.

At the back, an antique armchair sat under a small lattice arch that was draped with cobwebs. Art sat in the chair and opened his book. Again, lights hidden in the foliage near the ground created frightening shadows on his face. Thin clouds sailed past the new moon and added to the eerie lighting.

"Great effect," Max said.

Lil nodded. "The kids will love it. We better get back and get ready to work. We don't want to get fired on our first day."

Art laughed. "You son's a tough boss. I'll see you later."

The women returned to the front porch and took their places at the table. Max shivered a little at the effects of the mood lighting, bats swooping from the porch roof, and unearthly sounds all around them from hidden speakers. People came in pairs and groups up the path to the house. Some of the kids were in Halloween costumes even though Trick or Treat was still over a week away.

The special effects worked, based on the number of kids who clung to their parents' hands or hid behind them. The crowd continued throughout the evening and Max heard several kids ask parents if they could come back again. The haunted house project was a rousing success.

About halfway through the evening, a large thirty-something man came out on the porch, trailed by two young girls in full police uniforms. He carried a large bundle of black cloth. Max remembered selling him tickets earlier.

"Is Mr. Garrett around?"

Lil's mouth dropped open, and she stammered "Mr. Garrett?" Then she laughed. "Oh, I'm sorry! You mean Terry, my son." She hesitated and went on. "'Mr. Garrett' to me means my husband, Terry's father, and he's been gone for several years. It just took me back—" The young man began to look rather impatient. "I'm sorry. I'm babbling. I'll find him."

She hurried in the house to hide her embarrassment. Terry and Camille were in the kitchen, replacing a couple of burned out candles in the wall sconces.

"Terry, there's someone out front who wants to see you. I'm sorry—I didn't ask his name. A big man, has two little girls in police uniforms."

Terry laughed. "That's Josh Mansell, our new police chief. I noticed he has his girls dressed as patrolmen." He led the way back to the porch and Lil and Camille followed.

When they got outside, Terry made introductions. "Josh, this is my mother, Lillian Garrett, and my aunt, Max Berra. Max—Josh Mansell is our new police chief."

Josh nodded at each of them. "Nice to meet you." He held up the bundle of black cloth. "The girls found this behind one of the doors upstairs."

"We were investigating," the older girl said with a little swagger.

Josh carefully unfolded the bundle and held up a nun's habit with a large white collar.

Camille gasped.

"What? What's wrong?" Terry asked her.

Camille recovered herself and gave a weak smile. "It just reminded me of a robbery we had at the bank, maybe five years ago? The robber was dressed like a nun. He— or she—was never caught."

"I wasn't here then," Josh said, "but Dave Bender was, and he's told me about it. That's why I wondered if you knew why this was up there."

"You mean, you think this is actually the one the robber wore?" Camille asked. "I don't remember if this house was empty then or not. It's probably been about that long, but I would have to check the records. It was part of an estate, and the bank was the executor. There were no heirs, and the rest of the estate went to the library. But we could never get the house sold."

Terry said, "We were in such a hurry to get the house ready that we didn't pay much attention to the closets unless we needed to hide something in one."

"What is the white dust all over the habit?" Max asked.

Chief Mansell looked at the garment. "Plaster dust, I think. There are lots of places in the closets where plaster has fallen. We'll compare this against the security tapes of the robbery and see if it looks like the same one." He smiled at Terry. "Other than that, it's a great haunted house."

At 9:30, Terry appeared on the porch.

"Time to close up. I'll turn off the lighting and sound equipment. How did it go?" He eyed the moneybox that Max was sorting and counting bills into.

"The turnout has been fantastic," Lil said. "How did the kids do?" During the evening, Ren and Rival had curled up in bunk beds in the playroom disguised in white make up, and jumped out as people walked around the room.

"I think they had the time of their lives. Nothing better when you're a kid than scaring the bejeezus out of adults."

The screen door slammed, and a small but firm voice said, "I don't think you should say that word, Dad." Ren, her hair and face covered in grayish-white powder, looked up at him with the sternness of a reform school matron. Several of the adults hid their smiles.

Rival was right behind her. Terry decided distraction was the best course of action and said, "Why don't you help Granny Lil and Aunt Max put their table and money box away?"

The kids folded chairs and the table.

"Rival scared his girlfriend," Ren teased.

"She's not my girlfriend!"

"Is so. Is so. An' ya know what, Granny Lil? You can make a really weird noise if you blow across the edge of a piece of a paper."

Rival dragged one of the folding chairs toward the door. "We need some candy or somethin' up there. We get hungry when we're working so hard."

"I'll ask the Board." Terry held the door for his son

"I don't think a board will help..." Rival's voice trailed off as he disappeared into the house, the metal chair still clanging on the floor.

Art Carnel followed Rival back out to the porch. He whipped his cape around in front of him and twirled an imaginary mustache. "Success! The audience laughed, they cried, they screamed, they were at the edge of their seats--or they would have been if they were sitting down."

"Great!" Terry said. "I heard lots of good comments. Kids, time to get in the car. We'll have another big night tomorrow night so we need to rest up. Your mom already left and I believe she has treats ready at home."

The kids whooped and raced for the car

Max and Lil both dozed off on the ride back to Terry's in spite of the children's excitement.

As promised, Melody had cups of hot chocolate and monster cookies ready for them on the porch. Ren and Rival took center stage, as usual, with their accounts of the successful night. Max and Lil said their goodnights and were only too pleased to head to their comfortable quarters.

MAX WOKE THE NEXT day with Rosie's hot breath in her face. She rolled over and looked at her watch. It was an hour past her usual wake-up time—no wonder the dog was getting concerned. She pulled on a sweat suit and sneakers and led Rosie out the back door into the yard. The dog got her chores done and then broke into her 'crazy dance.' She leapt and whirled, snapping at imaginary nemeses in the air. She finally loped aback to Max and looked at her expectantly.

"It's a good thing you're beautiful, girl, because you sure don't have much for brains. You'll have to wait until my bathroom chores are done and then we'll go for a walk."

At the word 'walk', Rosie's ears went up, and she cocked her head.

"Not now," Max said and led the dog back inside. By the time she came out of the shower and redressed, Lil was up and ready for the day. Rosie pranced to the door and back until Max opened the door to the porch. She could hear voices in the kitchen so headed that direction. Melody and Terry supervised an eager Rival as he flipped pancakes at the stove.

Lil had followed. "Wow, Rival, you're cooking breakfast?"

"Yup." He had a large denim apron on already covered with grease spots and batter. Max would have been willing to bet that it did not look like that when Melody put it on him.

"Do I have time to take Rosie on a little loop around the neighborhood?" Max asked.

Melody rolled her eyes. "I think you have *plenty* of time. We're putting the finished pancakes in the warmer anyway."

"Can I go with you?" Ren asked.

"Sure. It's kind of chilly so you'd better get a jacket."

By the time Ren returned, Max had the leash hooked to Rosie's collar and they exited the front door. As they went down the front walk, Ren asked "Can I hold the leash?"

Max hesitated. "You can try. She's strong and if she tries to take off, you may not be able to hold her. She's pretty good most of the time."

Things went well for a while. They walked back down to the creek and watched the water. Rosie located a toad hiding in the rocks. Max pulled the dog back while Ren crouched down to examine the toad.

The loop included a small park and playground. But on their way back, a gray squirrel raced across the sidewalk, and Rosie bounded after it, jerking Ren's arm. Max managed to grab the leash just in time and, along with a command in a firm voice, convinced the dog that the squirrel was not in the cards today.

"We'd better head back or we'll miss the pancakes," Max said, and Ren readily agreed.

It was a quiet morning after breakfast; everyone seemed a little bleary-eyed. Terry had to work since the bank was open Saturday mornings. He arrived home at noon to find them all quietly occupied on the porch.

"What a well-behaved bunch. Mom and Aunt Max, Camille asked if you would be interested in a ride in the country this afternoon? It's a great day, and there's some drives around here that are particularly beautiful this time of year."

Lil smiled. "How thoughtful of her. I'd love to. Max?"

Max considered. "Why not?"

"She said she would pick you up at 1:00 unless we call and tell her differently. I'll get some lunch going," Terry said.

"I'm going to change." Lil closed her magazine and got up. Max soon followed.

CAMILLE DROVE A SMALL SUV. Lil took the passenger seat and Max got in back.

"We'll drive up north to the little town of Harvest. They're having an apple festival today and will be selling homemade apple butter, pie, caramel apples — everything apple you can think of."

"Yum," Lil said. "This is so nice of you."

Camille laughed. "Nothing like a road trip with a couple of interesting women, right?"

Max leaned forward. "Camille, have you always lived in Burnsville?"

"No, I grew up in Pittsburgh. I went to Vassar and got a job in a New York bank. I met my husband there, but the marriage didn't last. After the divorce, I wanted out of the city. Took my maiden name back and the job here. That was twenty-five years ago, and I love it here. Totally different life."

"I don't mean to be nosy," said Lil, which Max knew was exactly what she meant to be, "but is Art a serious relationship?"

Camille didn't seem offended. "I think not as much as he would like. But he's a fun companion. And he's as loyal as a new puppy. But I'm perfectly happy with my life the way it is."

"Did you hear anymore from the police about the nun's habit?" Max asked.

Camille grew serious. "Yes, Chief Mansell called this morning and said it looks like the same style." She shook her head. "It's really odd—not a clue in all of these years and then that turns up. I did check the bank records, and the house has been empty that long."

They discussed jobs and families the rest of the drive, taking breaks to admire the fall colors. Camille pulled over twice at lookouts so that they could snap some photos.

Max commented after one such stop, "It always amazes me how much of this country is wooded. Coming originally from the plains of southern Minnesota where trees are the exception, I love these drives."

They drove into Harvest and found a parking spot on a side street near the busy downtown area.

Vendors lined the street under colorful canopies. The smell of spicy cooked apples wafted through the air. Banjo music came from the other end of the block accompanied by clapping and foot stomping.

They wandered along, tasting apple treats, touching handcrafted items, and listening to mountain music. Camille was a pleasant and informative companion. Lil purchased a rag rug in shades of red and gray, and Max found a hand-knit sweater to her liking. Max had just purchased a caramel apple when Camille pointed out a little quilt shop on a side street.

"I'm not a quilter, and they probably wouldn't let me in with this anyway." Max waved the apple on a stick. "I'll just wait for you on this bench. Don't hurry."

41

She sat on a small iron bench overlooking Main Street and settled in to watch the people. A juggler in a clown costume held court with a group of kids and adults in the middle of the street. Dozens of people sat at picnic tables under a large open tent devouring apple pancakes being cooked by one of the community service groups. Off to the side, a woman dressed in a colonial costume demonstrated to several interested watchers how to make an apple head doll.

Max savored the sweet caramel and tart apple of her own treat, frequently licking her lips and fingers, while trying to keep from dripping the caramel on her pants. As she tilted her head to one side in an effort to stop a large glob of caramel from falling, she caught sight of a familiar face.

Art Carnel stood at the back of the crowd around the juggler, and hanging on to his arm was a redheaded woman. She pointed at the juggler, said something to Art and giggled, then buried her face in his arm. Maybe Art wasn't as loyal a puppy as Camille believed.

Max glanced back at the side street. No sign of Lil and Camille yet. Perhaps the woman was a sister or close cousin? She shouldn't jump to conclusions.

Max finished the apple and wrapped the stick in her napkin. After she threw it in a nearby bin, she turned back to the juggler crowd. Art Carnel was whispering in the redhead's ear. Max shrugged and walked over to a rack of apple festival sweatshirts. As she picked one out, she noticed Lil and Camille coming toward her, both with large shopping bags and laughing. She glanced over her shoulder again at the juggler but saw no sign of Art.

"Looks like a successful visit."

Lil opened her bag to display a kaleidoscope of fabrics in bright citrus colors. "I need to do a quilt for Ren. I made Rival a Star Wars one a couple of years ago, but haven't done one for her. I'll show you the pattern when we get back to the house."

Max nodded. "Nice. What about you?" She turned to Camille.

"Wellll…" she pulled open her bag. Blues and browns in geometrics and plaids predominated. "I'm going to make a lap quilt."

"Great colors," Max said.

"It's for Art," Lil said in a singsong, teasing voice.

Max's eyebrows went up. "I thought it wasn't a serious relationship."

"It isn't," Camille insisted. "I would do the same thing for any friend. I have, in fact. I really enjoy quilting but don't have any kids or grandkids, so I do them for friends."

Max pursed her lips and nodded. There wasn't much she could say to that; it made sense. She wouldn't mention seeing Art with the redhead.

THE BUSY EVENING was a repeat of Friday night, working at the haunted house. The wind picked up just enough to cause the bare branches in the tallest trees to creak and rub in protest, adding to the atmosphere.

Again, a good crowd took advantage of the dry weather to visit—many of them repeat customers whom Max recognized from the night before. As they were finishing up, Camille Bamford came up the sidewalk. "Is Terry around?"

"He's usually in the living room, seeing who he can scare," Lil said. "Is something wrong?"

"No, just a change of plans." Camille helped put pencils and entry slips for the drawing back in a box. "The bus tour that was coming Monday afternoon will actually be arriving tomorrow and staying at the bed and breakfast outside of town. They wondered if they could tour tomorrow night instead, since the effects are much better at night. I'll talk to him. Maybe we could shorten the public hours and give them a special tour at nine o'clock."

They carried the supplies and chairs into the house. Terry was turning off the lights and remotes. Camille explained the situation.

Terry pulled a printed schedule out of his back pocket and opened it. "I don't see why that wouldn't work. We might need our volunteers to stay a little later than usual." He raised his eyebrows and looked at his mother and aunt.

"No problem," Lil said and then grinned. "As long as we get naps in the afternoon."

"I think we can arrange that."

Melody had followed them in from the hall, resplendent in her witch costume and green makeup. "That's an excellent idea."

"Mel's always amenable to a nap." Terry hugged his wife with one arm. "At least if they're staying at the Inn, Wendell Welter should be mollified a little. He owns the Inn and was very opposed to the haunted house idea. Though it was tacky," He explained to Max and Lil. "And we want to keep him happy. The improvements to the Inn have really benefitted the town and tourism. He even got an award from the Chamber. So, I'll talk to the others who are still here, and call the rest of the volunteers in the morning."

"That'd be great." Camille smiled. "Thank you, Terry. I'll talk to you tomorrow."

Chapter Five

Max

SUNDAY DAWNED ANOTHER beautiful day. Max and Lil both slept in. When they got up, Rosie was absent from their bedroom and greeted them with her usual exuberance when they got out to the porch.

Ren jumped up and down. "Daddy and I already took Rosie for a walk! I tol' him not to let her chase any squirrels, din't I, Daddy?"

"Yes, it's a good thing you did, because she would have gotten away from me otherwise!" He patted Ren on her head.

Max got a cup of coffee and sat down at the table. The sunlight on the back yard was beautiful and peaceful. She was beginning to think she should add a 'scream' porch to her condo in Colorado. "So we have the big tour tonight. Anything else on the docket for today?"

"We'll be going to church at 10:30," Terry answered. "You are welcome to join us. Then we thought we'd get dinner at a nearby Amish restaurant."

"Let that be my treat," Max said. "I really appreciate your hospitality."

Terry grinned. "I would like to argue with you but my mom always said 'Just say thank you.' So, thank you."

"And Mother knows best." Lil set a basket of rolls and small plates on the table. "Ren, would you get some knives?"

"Sure!" Ren jumped down from her chair and raced to the kitchen.

"And don't run with them!" her grandmother called after her.

MAX ENJOYED THE SIMPLE service at a nearby Lutheran church. The restaurant served home-cooked food family style. Servers delivered platters heaped with roast beef and ham, bowls of mashed potatoes, sauerkraut, and fresh corn, and a crisp green salad. Ren whispered to Max that they also had 'very good apple pie with ice cream!.' They enjoyed that at the end of the meal.

They spent the afternoon relaxing on the porch and napping to prepare for the big evening. Max and Lil decided to get a little more in the spirit of the event.

"Ren, honey," Lil said, "Do you have any old costumes around?"

"Sure! We have a box upstairs. Rival and I can bring it down for you!" She dashed off to find her brother.

Lil shook her head. "I wish I had a tenth of that energy."

A few minutes later, they heard arguing and a box bumping down the steps. Rival dragged the box into the living room and Ren pulled the lid off.

"Ta-da!" she shouted.

"Is there anything in there that will fit us?" Max asked.

"Sure!" Ren was already pulling masks, unidentifiable apparel, and wigs out of the box. "Some of these are my mom and dad's." She grinned at them as if she was divulging a family secret.

Lil found a tangled gray wig in the pile and put it on. She struck a pose. ""What do you think?"

Ren clapped her hands. "Awesome, Grandma!" She pulled a cape, shimmering silver but wrinkled, from the box. "Try this on."

Lil whipped it over her shoulders with a flourish. "How about a mask?"

Ren pulled out a black eye mask. "This is a good one. You can be the Lone Ranger or a witch or—"

"I'm surprised you've heard of the Lone Ranger," Max said. "If you don't want it, Lil, I'll take it."

They continued to paw through the collection and finally each carried an armload to their suite and dumped them on the beds. After much trying on and preening in front of full-length mirror, they made their choices. Max opted for her black slacks and turtleneck, a red cape, the black mask, and a headband made of red and gold snakes fanning out in a crown.

Lil found a gray long dress in her suitcase and added the wig and the silver cape. She used makeup to produce finely arched brows, heavily outlined eyes, and dark streaks radiating from her eyes.

Max looked her over and laughed. "I can't decide if you look more like Kiss or a Goth."

"Either would be okay. But that headpiece is awesome. As Ren would say."

Max opened the door. "Let's go get an expert opinion."

Rival and Ren perched in chairs on the porch, knees up and thumbs beating a tattoo on handheld video game keys. Ren looked up first. "Wow! You guys look rad!"

Max looked at Lil. "Is that good?"

Rival scoffed. "Nobody says *rad* any more, Ren."

"I do." She stuck up her nose. "It means you look really great." Rival nodded his head vigorously in agreement.

Melody came out on the porch with a plate of sandwiches. "Wow! Is that stuff all from our costume box? I think I recognize some of it."

"It's our clothes, your accessories," Lil said. "I'm really excited about this evening. I feel like a kid again."

"Don't push it," Max said.

THE COSTUMES CREATED A STIR. Bert, one of Terry's co-workers at the bank said, "My wife tried to get me to dress up but I was too chicken. You ladies look great!"

Max looked around. "Is Art reading in the garden tonight?"

"Oh, I think so," Camille said. "I should probably check." She was soon back with a puzzled look on her face. "He's not out there. I hope he's not sick." She pulled out her phone and tapped a number. After a short wait, she put the phone away. "That's odd. No answer and no voicemail. Maybe after we get started, I'll check his apartment." She looked genuinely concerned.

The first part of the evening went quickly with plenty of customers. Laughs and screams echoed through the old house. Max and Lil continued to handle tickets until the time for the bus tour.

Camille returned after a search for Art, shrugging her shoulders. "No sign of him. I can't imagine him not calling at least."

She continued to look worried as they put away the ticket tables to get ready for the tour.

Terry walked out on the porch rubbing his hands together. "Good—glad you're getting things in order out here. The tour company paid for the whole group in advance so we don't have to collect ticket money. Mom, I would like you to be the 'host' in the kitchen. Here's a script that you can read or ad lib—whatever you're comfortable with. Aunt Max, how about the living room?"

"That's fine."

He handed a couple of sheets of typed paper to each of them and turned to Camille. "Any luck finding Art?"

"No. I'm worried."

"I'm sure there's a logical explanation." He scratched his head. "Aunt Max, would you consider reading the scary stories book out in the garden instead?"

Max nodded, the snakes on her head waving as she did so.

"I doubt if I can do it with as much drama as Art, but I'll do my best."

"Great. We'll split the group in two with about ten or twelve people each. And Camille, would you mind being the guide in the living room?" Terry asked. She agreed ,and Max handed her the script.

The back garden was quiet; the local customers had left, and the tour group wouldn't arrive in the garden until they had been through the whole house. Max could hear laughter and chattering coming from around the front of the house as apparently the bus unloaded its passengers.

The sounds made a surreal background to the silence of the garden, almost as if she was in a protected sphere. She walked slowly around the path with a flashlight, checking that all of the lights were on and admiring again the chicken wire dancers. A witch leaning on a tree had been knocked over so she set it up and made sure the spotlight below it was aimed correctly.

She rounded a corner and stopped short, her heart in her throat. A man's shoe protruded from under a bush and it appeared that there was a leg in the shoe. She screeched, turned to run back into the house for Terry, and then hesitated. Something wasn't right—the angle? The exposed skin? She moved closer and played the light over the limb.

She let out a deep breath as she identified the skin as plastic and saw that the appendage ended at the knee. A nudge with her foot put it back off the path and hidden enough to scare the people it was supposed to scare.

Her heart still pounded as she arranged herself in Art's chair and tried to even out her breathing before the tour reached her. The disconnect of the beautiful evening, the lighted trees, and the ghostly dancing figures with the spookier garden installations and sinister sounds from the wind in the trees kept her on edge.

Laughter and screams came out of the house as the tour moved through the rooms. Pulsing or colored lights visible through the windows advertised their progress. She leafed through the book and picked out two short stories to read to her guests.

Finally, Terry's voice cut through the garden. "This is the high point of our tour, the Haunted Garden. When you reach the back, you will find Medusa reading some bedtime stories." He cackled. Lots of excited chatter followed his speech and small groups began to move along the paths.

Max stood and moved into the shadows, unashamedly eavesdropping on conversations. Most of the tour members seemed to be her age or older.

Three women walked along one path, discussing a male tour member who was 'certainly free with his hands.' Other comments were interspersed with oohs and ahs over the white flowers proliferating in the garden. Two men discussed their golf scores and missed most of the scary spots. One man mentioned the story of the nun's habit; apparently Terry had passed it on in his introduction to the house and its history. Occasionally, startled squeaks followed by embarrassed laughter wafted through the garden.

As the first group neared her chair, Max sat again and opened the storybook. The stories were written for children, so Max expected that one of the children's stories would probably be enough for this group. She waited until ten or twelve had gathered around her.

"This story has been handed down for generations in these hills and people swear it's true. It was a dark, stormy night…"

One woman, perhaps a little younger than Max, listened thoughtfully and nodded. She had soft blonde curls and blue eyes that widened in alarm during the tense parts of the story.

When Max finished the story, she closed the book and gave an evil grin. "Any questions?"

Everyone in the group shook their heads and applauded. Several thanked her and someone said "Nice job!" They started to move away, but the blonde woman hung back.

Max tilted her head and waited.

The woman tittered a little, and almost blushed. "I just wanted to ask you about someone. Al Carson? Do you know him?"

Max frowned. "You mean someone from here? Burnsville?"

"Yes," the woman rushed ahead. "We met on a cruise and he was from here, but I haven't been able to get hold of him on his cell, and I don't see him in the phone book. He must not have a landline. So many people don't any more. I just thought you might know him."

"Oh, no. My sister and I are just visiting her son—my nephew—and we volunteered to help out here. We've only met a few local people."

Now the woman giggled. "I'm sorry. I just assumed… Great job on the story, by the way."

"Thank you. I'm just filling in for the guy who usually does it. Enjoy your trip!"

"Thank you." She moved on down the path as another group from the tour bus gathered to hear the story.

More applause greeted the end of the story, and the last group finally headed back to the bus.

Max closed her book and hoisted herself from the chair. When she got to the house, she turned out the garden lights. The last of the bus tour people were going out the front door and the volunteers gathered in the living room.

Camille brought out a couple of bottles of wine, plastic cups, a wedge of cheese, and crackers. Rival and Ren eyed the wine bottles with suspicion, and Camille said "Oops! I forgot. There're juice boxes in the kitchen refrigerator. Do you want to go get them?"

The kids raced to be first in the kitchen, accompanied by shouts and a little pushing.

Terry just shook his head and turned to the group. "Great effort tonight, folks. The tour guide was very impressed and she will recommend the stop for more groups." I think we're going to make a sizeable contribution toward the new auditorium."

The group broke into applause and chatter. A young blonde woman standing by Max leaned over and said, "You're Terry's mother? You must be very proud. He's done a great job."

"Actually, I'm his aunt—that's his mother over there in the gray wig— but we are both proud of him."

The blonde held out a hand. "I'm Denise Jansen, by the way. I'm one of the local dentists, but I've worked with Terry on the food pantry committee."

"Nice to meet you. Where were you working tonight?"

A man next to her, Vince something who Terry had said was a science teacher at the high school, said "Upstairs. She was my assistant. We had to keep that witch's cauldron in the bathtub bubbling."

They sipped their wine and traded stories about their patrons in each area.

A HALF HOUR LATER, they were in the car headed home.

"We got so many compliments as people left," Melody said. "They were really impressed."

Max sat forward from the front seat. "One woman asked me if I knew someone named Al Carson. She, of course, thought I was local. She said she met him on a cruise and thought he was from Burnsville. Do either of you know him?"

Melody shook her head and looked at Terry. "I've never heard the name. Have you?"

"No, and I know about everyone in town through the bank. Maybe she got the town wrong."

Ren, sitting between Max and Lil, bounced up and down. "We really scared one lady, didn't we, Rival?"

Rival, in the third seat, whooped. "We sure did! We thought she was gonna have a heart attack!"

Terry smiled, "Well, we don't want that. Then no one would come."

"But if she *died*, the house would *really* be haunted," Rival said.

"Let's change the subject," Melody said. "How about some popcorn when we get home?"

CHAPTER SIX

LIL

TERRY CAME HOME early on Monday. "A customer this afternoon said some of the signs on the lane are down at the haunted house. Kids, I suppose. I'm going out to set them back up so we'll be ready for tonight. It's starting to cloud up; we may be in for some rain. That'll probably keep the crowd down."

Lil closed the book she was reading. "I'll help." She looked pointedly at Max.

A big sigh. "Sure." Max hoisted herself up from the chaise lounge.

Lil rolled her eyes. "Don't put yourself out." It had been a long day. Lil figured they were both bored, and therefore crabby.

Terry looked from one to the other. "Really, I can handle it."

"Sorry I snapped. I need to do something." Max smiled faintly.

The sisters followed Terry out to his car, but despite Max's apology, the atmosphere was still a little tense. As they drove, huge black clouds rolled in from the west. They arrived at the entrance to the lane and got out of the car. Lil put her hand to her mouth. "Oh, my goodness!"

All of the signs had been knocked over into the lane. Most were bent and blown up against trees or under shrubs. The wind built, shaking loose leaves down and rattling branches. Lil looked up in alarm at a howl that came through the woods. The loose signs flopped and somersaulted as they rushed to pick them up.

Max brought two back to Terry, breathing hard. "Where are those kids of yours when we need them?" She winked. "The ground isn't as far away for them."

"True that." Terry laid all of the signs in the trunk. "I think we'll wait to put these back up when we leave. Maybe this will blow through. I want to check the house. Back in your chariot, ladies."

They drove up to the front of the house. The rain began with a vengeance. The screen door banged in the wind and the bats suspended from the porch ceiling whipped back and forth in a creepy life-like frenzy. Some of the fake cobwebs came loose and bunched together in non-life-like balls.

Terry grabbed a flashlight from the glovebox. "Follow me." He turned to look at them. "Unless you just want to wait here."

"We're with you." Lil pulled the hood of her raincoat up and opened her door. "I'm not staying here."

Max didn't say anything but followed right behind the other two. They hurried into the house to get out of the rain. The porch floor seemed creakier, and the inside door screeched in protest as Terry pushed it open.

"It wasn't locked," he said. "I wonder if I forgot last night." He hit the old style push button light switch. Nothing happened. "The power must be out."

He aimed his flashlight around the entry. A small table by the stairs was tipped over, and the beam picked out glistening pieces of glass scattered on the floor and three black silk roses lying in the shards.

Terry shook his head. "This isn't good." He opened the living room door and swept the light around the room. "Looks okay." They made the same checks of the dining room and kitchen and found no damage in either room.

"Do we need to check upstairs?" Lil asked.

"I don't know...it doesn't look like..."

Max interrupted. "Someone knocked the table over, and if they weren't headed into the other rooms down here, they must have gone upstairs. Why would anyone come in, knock over a table, and leave again?"

"You're right. We're here—we might as well check." He headed up the stairs, aiming the light down at the steps, so the women didn't miss their footing. Lil shuddered as she looked over her son's shoulder at looming darkness above them.

Max brought up the rear. "I hope they left the playroom alone. The kids would be crushed."

"You're right," Lil answered.

Terry reached the top and started to head toward the playroom, but turned instead toward the small bedroom at the top of the stairs. He pushed the door open with his left arm and shined the flashlight at the woman in the chair.

Lil peered over his shoulder and said, "I'm glad you took the axe out of her head."

Terry said nothing, just kept the light trained on the chair. He made a choking sound.

"Terry? What's the matter?" Lil looked up in her son's face.

"Mom, Aunt Max—maybe you should go back downstairs. No, wait, we only have one flashlight. Just stand over there." He directed them away from the bedroom door with his light. But Lil strained to see what he didn't want them to see and could feel Max pushing up behind her.

Lil said, "I don't understand. What is it, Terry?"

Max put her hand to her mouth. "It's a person, right? She was here last night with the bus tour."

Terry moved into the room with Max and Lil right behind him. He pulled out his phone as he neared the chair.

The woman wore the same white dress as the manikin had been dressed in and blood streaked her face., Unlike the manikin, her mouth was closed. Her eyes were open and seemed to emanate fear..

Max gritted her teeth, stepped forward, and gingerly felt the woman's neck for a pulse. She looked at the others and shook her head. "No pulse."

Terry gave the police their location. "There's a woman we believe is dead in place of one of the manikins

we had in this haunted house project. Okay. Thank you."
He hung up.

Terry took his mother's arm. "Let's go downstairs.
There are a couple of kerosene lanterns in the kitchen.
We're going to need more light."

Tears ran down Lil's face. "It doesn't seem right to
leave her."

"I know, but with one flashlight, we need to stick
together. And whoever did this could still be around."

Lil's mouth dropped open. She grabbed Max's hand,
and they followed her son down the stairs.

By the time Terry found the lanterns in one of the
kitchen cupboards and got them lit, they could hear
sirens nearing the house. Intense flashlight beams pierced
the darkness and rain, as heavy footsteps mounted the
porch. Terry opened the door.

"Come in, please." He stood back as three officers
entered, led by Josh Mansell. "Sorry to get you out in
weather like this, but I can't believe this has happened."

The chief nodded at the women and turned back to
Terry. "You said there's a dead woman here? A real one?"

Max wasn't surprised at his question. It would have
been her first response too.

Terry pointed up the stairs. "The room at the top of
the stairs. I need to call my wife and have her get the
word out that we won't be open tonight."

Chief Mansell nodded. "All right. An ambulance
crew should be here any minute just in case there's any
chance for her." He led the way up the stairs. His heavy-

duty flashlight lit up more of the stairwell, helped by those of the other two officers.

Terry got Melody on the phone and told her what they had found. He repeated it a couple of times; it was obvious that Melody was having a hard time grasping the news. Then they talked about how to best notify the public of the change in the schedule.

"Call Camille first; I'm sure she has some ideas. Becky Schultz sends out that chamber newsletter each week to all of the club presidents and others for them to share. Maybe she could use that list." A pause. "Okay, I'll call you after the police leave."

Another siren announced the arrival of the ambulance. Terry went to the front door to direct them.

Max and Lil stood in the kitchen around one of the lanterns, still in shock. The surreal event, the dim light, the indistinct voices and shuffling noises from upstairs all contributed to a pervasive chill.

Finally Max said, "I keep thinking how much worse it would have been if someone with small children had discovered that — her."

Lil shook her head and rubbed her arms. "It would have been Ren and Rival. They always go upstairs as soon as we get here. We were lucky that the problem with the signs brought us here early."

Terry came back in the kitchen and said to Max, "You recognized the woman?"

"I don't know her name, but she was with the bus tour last night. She's the person who asked if I knew a local man—I can't think of the name now—but I asked you about him last night. You said you'd never heard of him."

"Right. I can't remember the name either right now, but keep thinking." He scrolled through his phone. "Here's the name and number of the tour person—I need to write that down for the police." He opened another cupboard and pulled out a small notebook.

They turned toward the entry hall at the sound of heavy footsteps on the stairs. Chief Mansell walked into the kitchen, shaking his head. "I never expected something like this in this town. Do you know her?"

"No, but my aunt, Max, says she was in the bus tour group that came through here last night." He handed Mansell the slip of paper. "This is the name and number of the tour guide. You'll have to get her to make the identification."

Mansell looked up from the paper at Terry. "Do you know if they're still in town?"

"Yes. They were going to tour the brewery and the museum today and some of the shops tomorrow. They're staying at the Hilltop Inn."

The chief stuck the paper in his shirt pocket. "We'll have to call in the state crime lab. We're not equipped to handle something like this. Can you keep the house off limits until then?"

"Yes. I'm not sure we'll even want to open again. The board will decide, I think."

"Who has keys?"

"I do, of course, and Camille Bamford." He ticked names off on his fingers. "Patsy Johnson, the school liason. Art Carnel. Tom Muller. Trish Yoder. That's it."

"Would you make a list of those people? I will need to check and see if they all have theirs and if any of them were here today. And I'll need a key to the house."

"I'll do that. You can have my key and we'll get out of here so that you can lock up when we leave." Terry pulled the key off a ring and handed it to the chief. "Is there anything else?"

"Just a couple of other questions." Mansell turned to Max. "You visited with this woman?"

"Very briefly." Max explained about taking Art's place reading in the garden. "When I finished, she asked me if I knew a man from Burnsville whom she had met on a cruise. She assumed I was local, you see. I told her I was only visiting and knew very few people here, but when I asked Terry later, he had never heard the name either."

Josh Mansell raised one eyebrow and pulled a note pad and pen out of his pocket. "What was the man's name?"

Maxine shrugged. "We were just talking about that. Neither of us can remember. Sorry. Anyway, then she left."

More footsteps on the stairs signaled the ambulance crew removing the woman's body.

Chief Mansell conferred with the other two police officers.

One raised a large camera. "Difficult to get good pictures with the power out. Benton finally got a big spotlight out of the car so we're okay."

"Good," Mansell said. He nodded at Terry, Max, and Lil as they went out the front door.

Terry started the car but didn't put it in gear. Thunder crashed around them and the wind still howled.

He wiped the raindrops off his face. "Wow. I didn't know the woman, but it's a horrible thing. She probably has family and friends, wherever she's from, but all I can think of right now, is how am I going to tell the kids?" He looked across at Lil.

She patted his hand and said, "Maybe Mel already did."

CHAPTER SEVEN
MAX

BUT MELODY HADN'T. "I just told them we wouldn't be open tonight because of the weather." She looked at Terry apologetically. "I wimped out."

"That's fine." He hugged her. "We'll figure something out together. Where are they?"

"Upstairs watching a video. So who is this woman? Do you know?"

"No," Max said. "Remember last night when I asked if you knew some man from Burnsville. Neither Terry nor I can remember the name. The woman who died is the one who was asking."

"Oh, you mean Al Carson?" Melody asked.

Max snapped her fingers. "That's it. How did you remember that?"

"It made me think of Al Carstenson, who was in my high school class," Melody said. "But I've never heard of Al Carson. You said she met him on a cruise?" Melody asked Max.

"That's what she said. I'm thinking maybe he was a sleaze who gave her a fake name and town."

"I wondered about that, too," Melody said.

Terry got out his phone. "I should give that name to Mansell. Maybe someone in her group knows what cruise line, and they could track him down. Kind of suspicious that she starts asking about a non-existent person and then is found dead." He put his phone away. "Voicemail. I think I'll drive to the Inn. I'm sure that's where the chief is, and I should also express condolences to the tour group on behalf of the bank."

Max said, "I'd like to ride along."

Terry raised his eyebrows. "Doing a little sleuthing? I heard you were solving murders at the reunion last summer."

"Murder. Singular. And I didn't solve it on my own. Your mother helped. But seriously, I think it must be a terrible shock. Sometimes people become pretty close on those bus trips."

Lil said, "I'll go too. Is that little bakery still open? We could pick up some treats for them."

Terry looked at his watch. "They would be closed by now. Besides, the Hilltop Inn, where they're staying, has the best-baked stuff in town. Let's just go express our sympathy."

The wind was still howling and rain lashed the sides of the house. Terry had pulled his car in the garage so they didn't have to go back out in the weather, and when they arrived at the Hilltop Inn, they were able to park under the portico. They still hurried to the door to minimize drenching by what seemed like sideways sheets of water.

The door opened into a traditional entry hall with a wide staircase. A stooped man in a too-big flannel shirt looked up in surprise as he was about to turn into a double doorway carrying a tray of coffee cups. He seemed somewhat feeble and unassuming; Max was reminded of the many nervous characters played by Don Knotts. Yet incongruously, he appeared to have broad shoulders under the shirt. His face was pleasant and unemotional, and he squinted in their direction.

"Oh, Terry! It's you, isn't it? Come in and get those wet things off." He set the tray down on a sideboard and reached for their coats. A hall tree in the corner provided space for the dripping garments.

"Mother, Aunt Max—this is Wendell Welter, the owner of the Hilltop. Wendell, my mother, Lil Garrett and my aunt Maxine. I assume the bus group has gotten the bad news?"

Wendell picked up the tray again. Max noticed his hands shook. "They're in the living room. Chief Mansell arrived a little bit ago and told them. Such an awful thing." He shook his head and then almost got a smirk on his face. "I told the Chamber I thought the haunted house was a bad idea. I was right." He led the way through the double door.

People stood or sat in groups, hugging each other, patting others on the back, and shaking their heads. Several women cried visibly. Chief Mansell stood in one corner with a pad and paper talking to a thin well-dressed woman, who Max recognized as the tour director.

The chief looked up at Terry and the women as they entered and motioned them over.

The tour director gave Terry a thin smile. "Do you know yet what happened?" Her tone held suspicion.

Terry shook his head. "We have no idea. It was a shock to us all."

Chief Mansell said, "Maybe you and I could find a little more privacy to talk to Ms. Tarrington. Wendell, could we use one of the other rooms?"

Wendell, who had been setting up the coffee cups by a large chrome pot nearby, nodded. "Of course. Follow me."

Max and Lil moved out of the way. "I don't think we were invited," Lil muttered.

"Definitely not. But we can certainly talk to the others." Max led the way to three women standing by the window, one dabbing at her eyes with a wadded up tissue.

One woman said, "Oh! Aren't you the one who read the stories in the garden last night?"

Max wasn't sure whether the comment was just an observation or an accusation, but she would assume the former. She was also surprised to be recognized without her snake headdress. "Yes, I was. We wanted to tell you how horrified we are at what happened." She held out her hand and, to her surprise, the woman took it.

"Mary Carmody. We are all in shock, as you can imagine. Barbara was such a friendly person."

"Did you know her well? I hope they were able to notify her family." Max said.

A short stocky woman in an Ohio State sweatshirt, said, "She had a sister. Bonnie, I think was her name. Barbara was from Cincinnati. But I never heard her talk about any other family. I'm sure Marge has emergency contact information."

"Marge?" Lil asked.

"The tour director."

Mary looked at the other two, and then said, "I'm sure she wasn't married. She talked about contacting a man here in Burnsville that she'd met on a cruise."

Max nodded. "Yes, she asked me about him, but I'm not local either. We're just visiting. I couldn't tell her anything."

Mary shook her head, perplexed. "It seems like there's a lot of strange connections with that old house. Someone was talking at breakfast this morning about that nun's habit they found—said it was connected to bank robbery years ago?"

"The police think it might be." Max tried to redirect the conversation. "Was Barbara with your group at all today?"

Mary nodded. "She went on the brewery tour this morning, but at lunch said she wasn't feeling well. So she skipped the museum this afternoon. We assumed she was staying here to rest."

The third woman, wearing a name tag that said 'Sheri,' said in a low voice, "She seemed to be fine this morning, and then she got a call at lunch right before she decided not to go to the museum. I wondered if she was meeting that guy she mentioned."

"How would she go somewhere? You travel on a bus, right?" Lil asked.

"Yes, but the inn owner gave us information on a local taxi service — kind of an Uber affair."

"I see," said Max. "Well, you have our sympathies. How long have you been on this trip?"

"Just since Friday," Ohio sweatshirt said. "We started from Dayton. So, three days. We're supposed to leave here Wednesday for Lancaster County."

"Tomorrow, we're supposed to visit some of the shops here," Mary said. "I read that there's a great quilt shop."

"I asked about that and it's out in the country in an old barn. The bus isn't going out there. We'll have to get a taxi," said Ohio sweatshirt.

"Oh, I'll have to check that out. My son must be keeping it a secret from me." Lil patted Mary on the arm. "I hope they find out soon what happened to Barbara, and that the rest of the trip goes much smoother."

"Thank you."

A couple stood to one side of the fireplace, scanning the room and occasionally whispering to each other. Each held a half-full glass of red wine, and the man regarded the others in the room with a sneer. Lil led Max toward them and held out her hand.

"Hello. I'm Lillian Garrett. My son works for the bank that sponsored the haunted house. We just wanted to tell you how sorry we are about your experience."

They both ignored her hand. The man said, "I hope your son's employer is ready for a few liability lawsuits."

"Lawsuits?" Lil's mouth dropped open and her eyes widened. "But they had nothing to do with Barbara's death."

"Really?" said the woman. "Well, the lack of security there was their responsibility. Now our trip is ruined."

Max studied the woman a moment and said, "So was Barbara's. Let's go, Lil."

They walked across the room to another group, and worked their way around the room to the door, making small talk and uttering what words of comfort they could. There were a variety of reactions but none as cold as the couple by the fireplace.

Terry came back in the room and spotted them. They headed toward him.

"Ready to go?" he asked.

Lil nodded. "Yes, I think it's time."

"Why is that?" He held the front door for them, and waved good-bye to Wendell.

Max described the behavior of the couple by the fireplace. "Otherwise, everyone's been very nice."

Terry looked shocked, and then said, "I suppose it's to be expected. I'll need to call Camille when we get home."

BUT CAMILLE WAS SITTING in his kitchen with a cup of coffee and a plate of cookies in front of her, talking to Melody. Her hair was messy, and she appeared to be wearing no make up. Terry had never seen her like that. Rosie was curled up under the table.

Camille jumped up when she saw him. "Terry! What an awful thing! Mel said you went to talk to the tour people?"

"I just felt I had to do something. Mansell was there talking to the tour director and I found out a little more about the victim." He paused. "But, Camille, they've found no sign of breaking and entering. Whoever did it must have had a key. And we have quite a few people with keys."

"Oh, dear. Do you really think — ?"

"I don't know what to think. This woman apparently had a 'friend' here whom she met on a cruise. Someone named Al Carson. But no one knows him. The whole thing is so brutal. The killing and then placing her somewhere that kids may find her…I just don't know."

"Did you ever find Art?" Max scratched Rosie's head, who had finally noticed that her mistress had returned.

Camille gave a little laugh that sounded forced."Oh, yes. He had called on a couple of clients about a hundred miles away and was so tired he fell asleep in his motel Sunday and didn't wake up to call us. He's on his way back now."

"Does he know about the murder?"

"No, I talked to him before Terry called. Why?"

73

"Just wondering," Max said. She remembered Art with the redhead on Saturday. What she was *really* wondering was what kind of 'calls' he made.

Terry pulled out a chair and sat at the table, absently grabbing handful of cashews from a bowl. "I need to contact everyone who has a key to the house and see if they still have theirs." He turned to Camille. "Would you want to check with Art? You may also want to contact the bank's lawyers. Aunt Max said one couple was making noises about lawsuits. Give them a heads up."

Camille pulled out her phone. "Sure. I'll check with Patsy Johnson too."

"Thanks." They both moved out of the kitchen to make their calls.

While Lil, Max, and Melody waited, lightening flashed outside while the rain drummed against the windows. It provided an eerie soundtrack to their dark thoughts.

Terry and Camille came back to the kitchen. "All keys are accounted for," he said.

"You're right, Terry, about the brutality, " Max said, "and I keep coming back to *why*? What's the point? Is there a message? Because otherwise, why not just murder the poor woman and leave her in the woods. Or along the road. Or in her car—wherever she was killed. I just don't get it."

"It must be a message—what other reason could there be to go to all of that work?" Camille said.

"But if it's a message — to who? Or whom. Whichever. Someone opposed to Halloween or haunted houses? Someone who hates the bank? Someone who just wants to scare the crap out of everybody?" Terry's reverie was interrupted by a pounding on the front door — and then, as if an afterthought, the doorbell.

He hurried to the entry followed by Rosie. He yelled up the stairs before he opened the door. "Back in bed guys!"

He came back to the kitchen followed by the police chief.

"Can I take your raincoat?"

Melody said to Terry, "The kids are still up?"

Terry hung the raincoat on a hook by the back door and turned back to the group. "Yeah, they were peeking through the railing trying to see who was at the door." He rubbed his hands together. "Now, Josh, would you like some coffee?"

"No, I just have a couple of questions. Did you find out about the keys?"

"Yes," Terry said. "Everyone has theirs."

"And none of them were at the house today?"

"No," Camille said.

"But the door was unlocked when we got there this afternoon," Terry said. "I thought maybe I forgot to lock it last night."

"Did you lock it?" Mansell asked.

"I thought I did, but I couldn't swear to it. We were pretty pumped about how well the tour went when we left last night, so I don't really know."

75

"The house looks like it was pretty grand in its time," Lil said.

"It was, but it's in terrible shape now. The roof leaks and most of the plumbing doesn't work. It would cost a fortune to restore and then the utilities would be astronomical. We just did some cosmetic stuff for this project." Camille shook her head. "Buyers just aren't interested in a house like that—not in a town this size. The plan now is to turn it over to the fire department for a practice fire after the haunted house is done and then sell the lot." She paused a moment. "Wouldn't that be something if the bank robber had been using it as a hideout?"

Chief Mansell said, "Meanwhile, we haven't found anything so far that would explain the murder or why the woman was there."

Terry nodded. "We were just talking about that—why the murderer went to so much work to display the victim. You don't think she was killed there, do you?"

"No, there's no sign of that. Or, so far, of the manikin that was originally in the chair. We can't find that either. Well, I'd better get back. I need to check on some things, and then I'm ready to get out of this weather and into my bed." He got his raincoat and put it back on, still dripping a little on the floor.

Terry walked him back to the entry and let him out. Back in the kitchen, Camille stood. "I need to get home too. Terry, we'll meet first thing in the morning and figure out some options for the haunted house project."

SHORTLY, LIL AND MAX had donned their pajamas and were propped in the twin beds, reading, not yet ready to fall asleep. However, Max couldn't concentrate on her book. She finally closed it and turned off her small bedside lamp.

As she lay staring up at the ceiling, she had a thought. "Lil, that woman—Barbara—was looking for someone named Al Carson?"

Lil stuck her finger in her book to hold her place and looked at her sister over the top of her reading glasses. "Yes. Why?"

"Al Carson sounds a lot like Art Carnel. Do you suppose he's the missing Cassanova, and he gave her an alias on the cruise? Lots of people use names with the same initials. Maybe he has monogrammed luggage or handkerchiefs or something."

"Well, of course we hardly know him, but would he risk what he has going with Camille to have a fling with someone else? I mean, Camille is rich and attractive and fun…"

Max interrupted and raised herself up on one elbow. "That's just it. I *know* that he would. Saturday at the apple festival, when you and Camille were in the quilt shop, I saw him watching the juggler. He had a clingy redhead hanging on his arm, giving him a nuzzle every once in a while. I don't think she was a sister or a cousin."

"You never mentioned it."

"I didn't want to in front of Camille, and later I forgot about it."

77

Lil sat up straight in the bed. Her book slid off her lap and onto the floor. "You mean, you think he's the murderer? That's why he hasn't been around?"

Max shrugged, lay back, and continued looking at the ceiling, as if the answer was there somewhere. "It's possible. Maybe he didn't want Barbara to mess up his thing with Camille." She sighed. "He doesn't even seem like that great of a catch."

Lil picked her book up and put it on the nightstand. She turned off her own light. "He was personable when we had lunch with him but, I agree—it's hard to imagine women fighting over him. It shouldn't be too hard to find out if he's been on a cruise lately. Or any kind of vacation. Do we know when Barbara was?"

"That Mary Carmody who we spoke to tonight knew about the cruise. Maybe Barbara mentioned to her when it was. We need to talk to those people again tomorrow."

"We could call and offer them a ride to the quilt shop! But, we have to be very subtle about this so we don't get Terry in trouble. Maybe *he* can find out if Art has done a cruise, though."

"You know me," Max smiled in the dark. "The model of discretion."

Lil snorted. "Good night."

CHAPTER EIGHT
MAX

THE NEXT MORNING, the mood on the Garrett porch was a little lighter, partly because the storm seemed to have worn itself out, leaving only dripping trees and mud puddles. Ren couldn't resist jumping in a few when she and Max took Rosie for her morning walk. Rosie thought it was a wonderful idea, and managed to soak both herself and Ren.

When they returned to the house, Melody turned from the sink and covered her mouth at the sight. Terry looked to see what her alarm was about. Ren stood there with muddy drips running down her face, some of her red curls dangling limp with more brown tones than usual, and a smear across the arm of her yellow windbreaker.

Ren saw her mother's face. "It was Rosie's fault. *She's* such a mess, she had to stay in the garage!"

Melody held back a smile with effort and put her hands on her hips. "Rosie doesn't have to go to school in twenty minutes. Another shower for you." She pointed to the stairs.

"Aw, Mommy," Ren began, but then caught sight of her father coming around the island. "Nooo!" she screeched and raced up the stairs giggling, with Terry right behind her.

Mel shook her head and leaned on the island. "I don't like gender stereotyping, but I don't think little boys scream so shrilly and enjoy it so much."

Rival looked up from his bowl of cereal. "That's for sure."

"Oh hush, Mr. Big Ears," his mother said.

Lil nodded. "You're right. Little girls have weaponized screaming. Terry's sister could almost break glass. But I'm sure Max and I were never like that." She grinned.

SHORTLY AFTER, TERRY returned downstairs with a scrubbed Ren in tow. Melody loaded the kids in her car for the ride to school, while Terry refreshed his coffee and sat down at the counter.

"I'm not looking forward to meeting with Camille this morning. We need to make a decision about whether to open the haunted house again. If we don't, it's going to put a big hole in the auditorium budget. If we do, some people will think it's disrespectful to the dead, and we might not take in much money anyway."

Max nodded. "It's a shame on so many levels. Your mom and I were talking last night about the elusive Art Carnel."

"Camille said she finally heard from him."

"Yes. We know. But Art Carnel sounds a lot like Al Carson—the man Barbara was looking for. She said she met him on a cruise and he lived in Burnsville. Yet none of you have ever heard of him. Is Art the type of guy who might give a woman a fake name on a cruise? And do you know if he's been on a cruise recently?"

"Oh, come on." Terry added a packet of sweetener to his coffee and stirred it. "Art's a nice guy. A little pushy about his investment business, perhaps, but he worships Camille. He wouldn't do anything to upset her."

Max raised her eyebrows at Lil, who nodded. "I'm not sure that's true." She told him about seeing Art and the redhead in Harvest.

Terry wiped his hand across his face. "Wow. I never would have thought that. Harvest isn't that far away. You would think he would be more careful."

"Terrance Garrett!" Lil said. "Are you saying his sneaking around on Camille is okay if he doesn't get caught?"

Terry held his hands up. "No, no, Mom. You raised me better than that." He laughed and tweaked her cheek. "I just meant that if he bothered to give a fake name out in the middle of the ocean, you would think he'd be more cautious around here. But I still can't believe it. Are you saying you think he's the *murderer*?"

"I don't know," Max shrugged. "It's just odd, that's all. Do you know, or can you find out, if he's been on a cruise and when?"

"Probably. Do you know when Barbara's cruise was?"

"No." Lil winked at Max. "But we know a couple of ladies on the tour who need a ride out to a quilt shop that's in an old barn. If you tell us where it is."

"Quilt shop? Actually, I don't hang out in those much. When Mel comes back, she can probably give you directions."

"Do you have a local phone book, Terry? I'll call the Inn and make arrangements with Mary Carmody and her friend," Max said.

Terry obliged and when Melody returned, Lil wrote down directions to the quilt shop.

"I would love to go with you, but today is my day to help with Meals on Wheels," Melody said. "I want to learn to quilt."

Max laughed. "You'll have to talk to your mother-in-law about that. My sewing expertise is limited to replacing buttons."

"And that's iffy," Lil said. "I will be glad to teach you quilting, but we have an ulterior motive here. The women we are taking knew Barbara, the victim, and we want to pick their brains."

Melody grinned. "Here I thought you were just being nice. Have a good day anyway."

BY THE TIME they stopped at the Hilltop Inn, all signs of the previous day's storms had disappeared and 'October's bright blue weather' had burst forth in all of its glory. Mary Carmody waited on the porch with the Ohio sweatshirt woman, who Mary introduced as Cathy

Messer. Today Cathy wore a sweatshirt that said 'Ask me about my grandchildren.'

Max opened the door to the Studebaker and said, "I will warn you that my Irish Setter, Rosie, usually rides in the back, and her main talent is shedding. I tried to clean it up this morning, but I might have missed some."

Mary waved her hand in dismissal. "I have cats at home. I'm used to it. This car is *so* cool!"

"Oh, it is!" Cathy snapped a selfie with her phone. "My husband is going to be so jealous."

Once on the road, Cathy was full of questions about the car—how long Max had owned it, what she had done to it, and where she got it. By the time Cathy sat back in the seat out of breath, Lil said, "I think this is our turnoff coming up on the right."

They made the turn. Max said to her guests, "So how well did you know Barbara? And by the way, what was her last name? I never heard."

Mary said, "Her last name was Gunter. Of course, we just met her at the beginning of the trip so we didn't know her well."

Max debated how to diplomatically bring up Barbara's love life and the cruise, when Lil said, "So what do you think about this guy she met on a cruise? Was he just stringing her along?"

"Welll," Cathy looked sideways at Mary, "We talked about that, Mary and me. There's lots of guys on those cruises looking to separate a widow from her money."

"She was a widow?" Max asked.

"Yes. I think she said her husband died about two years ago," Mary said.

"This must be it!" Lil pointed at a large dark red barn trimmed in crisp white with a gravel parking lot in front of it. A sign in the peak bore a painted 'Flying Geese' patchwork design and the name 'Quilt Barn' in block letters.

Discussion of Barbara Gunter ceased as the women got out of the car and headed in a screen door.

"Good Morning!" A short woman with blonde, frizzy hair looked up from behind a wide wooden counter at the back. She was cutting squares of a variety of orange print fabrics. "Is this your first time at the Quilt Barn?"

Max walked toward her. "Yes it is. Two of these ladies are on a bus tour and my sister and I are visiting her son." She turned to indicate the others and found no one behind her. All three still stood near the door, their mouths open, as they slowly took in the kaleidoscope of colors. Fabric bolts marched around the structure five shelves high. Multicolored quilts hung above the shelves on the walls and from the center beams. Max hadn't even noticed.

She turned back to the woman and grinned. "I guess they like it."

The woman smiled back and placed another bolt on top of the stack on the counter. "I take it that you're not a quilter?"

"No, I'm not. I just appreciate others' work."

The woman spoke over Max's shoulder to Lil, Mary, and Cathy. "We have a twenty percent off sale today on fall fabrics—everything on that east wall. There's hot cider and gingersnaps on that table in the corner. Let me know if I can help you with anything."

"I think we're all just browsing, but this will be hard to resist," Lil said.

Max followed Mary Carmody around a display of flannels. "Do you make a lot of quilts?"

"Mostly small wall hangings. I'm looking for something for my niece's nursery—she's expecting a little boy in about six weeks."

"How nice. Getting back to Barbara a minute, did she ever say when she went on that cruise?"

"I don't remember for sure, but she talked about it a lot. She—oh, look at this print with Scotty dogs and the companion pieces! My niece and her husband plan to name their baby Scott. Maybe I should do a crib quilt instead of a hanging. I can't believe how cute this is, and the colors are perfect." She pulled three bolts in blues and greens out of the display. "Would you bring that solid blue and the one with the green and black stripes?" Mary marched back toward the counter, bearing the bolts in her arms.

Max tugged at the bolt of blue fabric and managed to work it loose, but the striped bolt was wedged in tighter on another shelf, and the texture of the flannel created more friction. Frustrated, she gave it an extra jerk, and the whole row of bolts tumbled to the floor.

Lil rushed over and started picking them up. "What *were* you doing?"

"Mary asked me to bring two of the bolts that she couldn't carry. But one was stuck." Max felt like a whiney little kid making excuses—which made her mad. She had tried to help.

Lil stood the bolts on end that she had picked up but when she leaned over to get more, they fell over again.

Cathy motioned the clerk over.

"Oh, my!" She clapped both hands to her face. Then she giggled. "No harm. I'll get it later. They need to be in order by color and shade."

Lil said, "We can at least pick them up off the floor and stack them where you can get to them." She laid two bolts on a side table.

"I'm so sorry," Max said.

The clerk waved a hand. "Don't worry about it. Fortunately fabric doesn't break. Which are the other ones that your friend wanted, do you know?"

Max grabbed the blue and the striped fabric. "I'll bring them up." Lil and Cathy went to work stacking the wayward bolts.

The clerk asked Mary about the niece's baby, her plans for the fabric, and other similar projects she had done. She measured off batting and added several spools of thread to the stack.

Lil and Cathy picked up all of the bolts off the floor, and brought their own choices of fabric to the counter. They chattered excitedly between bites of cookie and sips of cider. Max drummed her fingers on the counter, absently thumbed through a rack of instruction books, and checked her watch. Finally the purchases were done and bagged.

They returned to the car and Max opened the trunk to stow the bags. "Thank you so much for bringing us out here," Mary gushed.

"No problem," Max said. "I hope somebody remembers the way back to town."

"Got it," Lil said, holding up her phone. Once in the car, she gave directions over the voices of the two women in the back seat, who discussed their projects and any other possibilities in the barn that they had passed up.

"I'm thinking I need to bring my quilt group over here for just a day trip," Cathy said. "It really isn't that far."

"Great idea," Mary agreed.

"Turn right up here," Lil told Max, and pointed ahead to a tee intersection. "Then there's just that short curvy stretch back to the blacktop. Easy-peasy after that."

Max made the turn and they started down a winding road. The trees overhanging the road were aflame with color, with a backdrop of cobalt blue sky. The little Studebaker took the curves handily. Max relaxed into the drive and waited for a break in the chatter to ask more about Barbara Gunter.

As they approached a farm entrance on their left, a squawk and a flurry of feathers startled her out of her reverie.

She braked the car and it skidded to a halt on the dusty gravel. "What was that?"

Lil pointed out the window at three dark red chickens scurrying to the side of the road. Max suspected the squawks were not compliments directed her way.

"Did I hit something?" She opened the door and got out; Lil did the same. The looked under the car and examined the grill. They only found a few feathers.

"It must have just been a close call," Lil said. They returned to the car.

Cathy and Mary leaned forward from the back seat. "Those are Rhode Island Reds," Cathy said. "I was raised on a farm."

"Me, too," Mary said. "Did you ever have those chickens attack you when you were gathering eggs? One time—" And the rest of the way into town, they traded stories about chickens.

After Max dropped them off at the City Center Cafe, where they were supposed to meet the rest of the tour group for lunch, she drove toward the bank.

"Well, that was certainly a bust! Every time I was going to ask them about when Barbara's cruise was, something happened. Mary finding that cute fabric, fabric falling over, chickens attacking my car... I can't believe it. I couldn't get a word in edgeways once they started to talk about chickens."

"Last May."

"Last May what?"

Lil grinned at her sister. "Barbara's cruise was last May. I asked Cathy when we were picking the bolts of fabric up. Cathy remembered because Barbara was very definite that she wanted to go before hurricane season."

Max held up her right hand for a high five. "Great goin', Sis!"

"You're welcome. Now let's hope Terry found out when Art was gone, if he was. By the way, Barbara also told Cathy that she had made some investments with 'Al Carson.' And she's never heard any more about them."

"So another motive. That's good to know."

"Do you really think Art is the murderer?"

Max shrugged. "There's an awful lot of coincidences involved. Art happens to be gone when Barbara's in town and reappears after she dies. Of course it depends on whether Al Carson and Art Carnel are the same person." She pulled in to the bank parking lot. "Let's go see what Terry found out."

CHAPTER NINE

MAX

TERRY WAS BENT over his desk in his office. He straightened when they entered. "How did your morning go?"

"It wasn't easy," Max said, "but we finally found out when Barbara took her cruise."

"*Who* found out?" Lil asked.

Max rolled her eyes with as much drama as she could muster. "Okay, your mother found out. Because I was busy lugging fabric and chasing chickens."

Terry smirked. "I'll ask about that later. I have some information too. Have a seat for a few minutes and then we'll go get lunch." He perched on the corner of his desk and held one wrist with the other hand. The stance reminded Max of a principal once when she was in fifth grade and had put glue on the teacher's chair.

"Are we in trouble?" she asked.

Terry burst out laughing. "Why would you say that?"

"Just the way you're sitting on the edge of your desk."

He moved back to the chair behind his desk. "That better? What did you find out?"

Lil smiled. "Barbara's cruise was last May."

Terry grew serious. "Huh. Art Carnel was gone at that time, too. Camille said he went to visit his brother in Michigan."

"That's what he told her, anyway," Max said.

"Yes. I still can't see him as a murderer, though."

Lil added, "Barbara had also made investments with 'Al Carson' and had never heard any more about them. Her friends weren't sure whether she was more interested in seeing this guy again or finding out about her money."

"Hmm," Terry said. "And then there's the bank robbery and the nun's habit."

Max frowned. "What possible connection could that have to the murder?"

"That is a puzzle," Terry agreed. "We're just wondering if the house was used as some kind of hideout in the past and maybe still is."

Lil frowned. "You said last night the robber was never caught. Was the money recovered?"

"No. We're considering the possibility that it could be hidden somewhere on the property. It's more likely that the robber has already spent it. The big question is why Barbara was there, or even near there. Or how she got there."

"Last night, Mary and Cathy said that they were given contacts for a taxi service in case they wanted to go somewhere on their own. Maybe you — or the police — can check with them and see if that service picked her up.

One of the women told us that Barbara left the group after lunch yesterday—claimed she didn't feel well."

Terry nodded. "The tour guide—Marg—told the chief and me that, too. She went back to the Inn, but no one saw her after that. Wendell said he didn't see anyone come back, but he was out doing some fall cleanup in his garden."

"How was she killed?" Max asked. "I haven't heard anyone say."

"Josh didn't say it was a secret, I guess. She was strangled. That high necked-dress covered up the marks."

Camille tapped on the door and opened it. "Excuse me for interrupting, but I would like to take you all to lunch at the Brat House."

"That would be great," Terry said. He turned to his mother and Max. "I usually have to buy, so we'd better take advantage of this."

Camille smiled. "I didn't say I'd buy; just that I would take you there."

Terry grabbed a jacket. "Great idea anyway, and we can compare notes on the case."

Camille's eyebrows went up. "On the case? Are you moonlighting as a detective now?"

"It's my mother's fault," Terry answered.

Lil laughed. "Everything always is, isn't it?"

Camille went to get her keys and purse.

Max asked Terry in a low voice "Should we tell her our suspicions about Art?"

Terry considered. "I think you should. Just be diplomatic, please?"

"Of course."

They joined Camille at her car.

"What is the Brat House?" Lil asked as they started out of town.

"A very popular place overlooking the river. Famous for their German food but they also have good steaks and fish."

"Doesn't sound like a light lunch," Lil said.

"It depends on if you have your pie a la mode or not," said Terry.

THE BRAT HOUSE sat at the edge of a bluff overlooking the river. It had rustic decor with windows all along one side. Camille spoke to the hostess, and a waiter led them to a table by the windows.

"This is beautiful." Lil pointed out the window. "Even a little waterfall." The river below the restaurant tumbled over rocks and wound through narrow chutes. Bright colored fall leaves dropped from the overhanging trees danced along, contrasting with the deep green of the pines marching up the opposite bank.

"It's my favorite spot," said Camille. The waiter approached with a bottle of Chardonnay, showed it to her, and poured a small amount in her glass. She tasted it, nodded, and smiled. He poured the others.

Max glanced over the entrees and the prices on the menu. She opened the snowy white cloth napkin and spread it in her lap, catching Terry's eye as she did so. She gave him a slight grimace as she thought about deflating Camille's opinion of her boyfriend as thanks for this lovely lunch.

Lil also perused the menu with an uncertain look on her face.

After they'd placed their order, Camille leaned forward and folded her hands on the table. "So what's happening with 'the case?' Should I have worn my deerstalker hat?" She grinned at them.

"I have a question—just curious about the bank robbery. Was there only one robber?" Max asked.

Camille shook her head. "Only one came in the bank, but there was a getaway driver. There were a couple of witnesses outside—it was a rainy day—and they didn't recognize the driver, but they did get a partial license plate number off the car. Ironically, by the time they identified the guy—a year or so later—he had already been caught and sentenced for another crime. He died in a prison fight. So they never got to question him. The money was never recovered."

Lil unfolded her napkin and placed it across her lap. "Wow. That's quite a story."

"Mother and Aunt Max have something else they want to talk to you about," Terry said.

So much for putting this discussion off, thought Max.

Lil gave Camille her most sympathetic and understanding look. "It's about Art Carnel."

"Oh!" Camille laughed. "*That* mystery is solved. Art was making some sales calls out of state. Didn't I tell you that?"

"Yes, you did. That isn't our question," Max said. "You know that Barbara Gunter, the murder victim, asked several people if they knew Al Carson—a man she had met on a cruise."

"Yes, I think I remember you saying that last night."

"We think Al Carson and Art Carnel may be one and the same person."

Camille sat back in her chair and her expression went flat. "What—what makes you think that?"

"It has to be investigated further," Terry put in. "We just have circumstantial evidence right now. The names are similar, both sell investments, and Art was out of town at the time Barbara met Al Carson on a cruise."

Camille said, "That's why you were asking me about Art's absences? That's *very* circumstantial. You might as well say they were both born on a Wednesday or both like peanut butter."

"Put like that, it sounds pretty flimsy," Terry admitted. "It's just that several people have said that Barbara was so certain that this Al Carson was from Burnsville, and yet no one here has ever heard of him."

Camille shook her head. "No. I see where you're going with this. You think that Art is the *murderer*?" Her shrill voice caused a few nearby heads to turn. "He's not like that. I don't want to talk about this any more." She turned to Lil and Max with a plastic smile. "Terry said you took a couple of women from the tour out to the Quilt Barn this morning. What did you think?"

"It's amazing," Lil said. "Except Max tried to tear the place apart." Over Max's protest, Lil told them about the fabric bolt fiasco with some embellishment. The story lightened the mood and Camille appeared to relax again. The rest of the lunch, Terry steered the conversation away from the murder, the bank robbery, and the haunted house to tales of his children's exploits and his own childhood in Kansas. Camille encouraged his stories by fielding interested questions about life in the Midwest.

They returned to the bank after lunch. Camille said a hurried goodbye, explaining that she was almost late for a meeting. Terry walked Max and Lil to Max's car.

"Well, that didn't go so great," Terry said, as he held the door for his mother.

"No, it did not," she answered.

Max leaned over from the driver's seat. "To my mind, she's a little too defensive. I'm not sure she has that much confidence in Art."

"You may be right." Terry leaned on the door. "But we don't have much to go on: initials and being gone at the same time."

"Careful of the paint," Max said.

Terry stood up and put his hands behind his back. "Ooops. Sorry. I wonder if Barbara Gunter had a picture of her on-board romance?"

"The police chief should be able to tell you. Wouldn't they have searched her room?"

Terry nodded. "I guess I should ask."

"Are you going to be in big trouble with Camille?" Lil asked.

"I don't know. She doesn't usually hold a grudge, and she always says her relationship with Art is not serious, but I'm not sure any more that's true. She *is* pretty defensive about him."

Max said, "We'll get out of your hair. I think we should visit a little more with our quilting friends. Maybe Barbara showed them a picture of 'Al.'"

Terry nodded, but was obviously distracted by Camille's reaction. "See you later." He slapped the fender of the Studebaker

"Watch the paint!" Max.

Lil cast a sideways look. "You'd think this car was your child."

"It is." Max eased the car away from the curb. "I think we ought to stop back at the Inn and talk to Mary and Cathy without the quilt shop distraction."

"I'm for that."

THEY STOOD IN THE ENTRY hall and were surrounded by total silence.

"Hello?" Max called out. "Mr. Welter?"

After a few moments, footsteps came from the kitchen and service area. The swinging door pivoted open and Welter shouldered through, drying his hands.

"Yes?" He didn't look as if he recognized them.

"I'm Terry Garrett's mother, Lil, and this is my sister Max. We were here yesterday afternoon…"

"Oh, yes. I'm sorry I didn't recognize you. I have some vision loss and in certain light... well, that doesn't matter. What can I do for you?"

Max said, "Two of the women on the bus tour rode out to a quilt shop with us this morning. We want to visit with them some more. Mary Carmody and Cathy Messer?"

Wendell continued to wring the towel in his hands. "Oh, I don't know anyone's name besides Marjorie Tarrington. The tour guide. She's been here before. But I haven't met any of the others."

Max looked at Lil, puzzled. She turned back to Welter. "Is anyone from the group here?"

"No, I don't think so. They all left on the bus."

"I see. So you hadn't met the woman who was murdered either?"

"No, no. I'm sure not. I did overhear one woman talking to someone on the phone yesterday after lunch. I think she was arranging to meet the person at the Kell house."

Lil frowned at him. "Did you tell the police that?"

He looked like he had said more than he intended. "No. I didn't know who it was. The woman was in the back garden on the other side of a hedge. I never did see her, and like I said, I never got anyone's names. Why are you asking all of these questions?"

"We're just trying to help the police," Max said, patting his arm. "We'll get out of your way." She grabbed her sister's arm and tugged her toward the door. "Thank you, Mr. Welter!" she called over her shoulder.

Once outside, Lil twisted free of Max's grip and rubbed her arm. "What was all the about?"

"He's not going to tell us anything—or he doesn't know anything—I'm not sure which. What do you think of Mr. Welter?"

Lil shrugged. "He's a bit strange. Why?"

"I don't know. It just seemed like he was awfully eager for us to know that he hadn't met anyone in the tour group. Kind of odd for a host, don't you think?" Max started the Studebaker. "And that bit about overhearing that conversation—do you think it was Barbara? Mary told us yesterday that Barbara came back to the Inn after lunch and was going to rest."

"It must have been her. It sounded like she was the only one who left the group. I think you're right about Welter being off. Why would he *not* tell the police about that conversation, especially since it involved the Kell house?"

Max considered that and nodded. "True. He's kind of strange physically, too. He looks like the stereotypical wimpy guy in a movie, but he doesn't really carry himself that way. You know what I mean?"

"Yeah. He's just an odd duck. Should we call Mansell about it?" Lil got out her phone.

"Definitely. That was a pretty big omission on Wendell's part."

Lil entered the number on Mansell's card. "Chief? This is Lil Garrett, Terry's mother. We thought we should pass on something Wendell Welter just told us." She explained the story that Wendell told them about the phone call in the garden. She paused at the end. Her face flushed a little. "Yes, I see. We thought you should know. Bye"

She punched off the phone and turned to Max. "Well. He says we shouldn't be interviewing people about the case."

"Is he going to check it out?"

"He didn't say. He sounded pretty annoyed. Well, we tried. We still need to contact Cathy and Mary. I got Cathy's cell number this morning. Should I call her and see where they are?"

"Yes—see if we can meet up with them and when."

Lil made the call, exchanged pleasantries for a minute and then made their request. "Just a minute. I'll see." She covered the phone. "They want to take us out for supper as thanks for taking them to the quilt shop."

"I'm game," Max said. "Did Terry and Melody have plans for this evening?"

"I doubt it. We all thought we'd be working at the haunted house." She turned back to her phone. "Cathy, can I call you back in a few? I need to check that my son and his family don't have plans for us."

More phone calls resulted in arrangements made for Max and Lil to pick the other two up for an early supper at a pizza joint in town. Meanwhile, Max and Lil decided they would return to Terry's house, walk the dog, rest a little, and help Melody out by picking the kids up from school. After the busy morning and stressful lunch, the respite was welcome.

Rival started the questions as soon as he got in the car. "My friend Dylan said the lady that died at the haunted house yesterday was *scared* to death! Is that true?"

"No," Lil said. "They don't know what happened yet."

Max noticed that she looked uncomfortable at her white lie.

Rival persisted. "Are we going to be open tonight?"

"I don't think so."

Rosie particularly was glad to spend some time with them. She got a long walk with Max, and then Ren begged to help with another walk. Rosie had no objection.

Finally, the sisters abandoned Melody to the noisy household and drove to the Hilltop Inn. Their passengers were waiting.

"Are you sure you just want pizza?" Mary Carmody asked when she got in the car. "We'd be happier to treat you to something fancier."

"It seems like we've eaten big meals constantly since we've been here. Pizza sounds just perfect," Lil said.

CHAPTER TEN
MAX

THE PIZZA PLAZA reminded Max of a cafe she had frequented in college. In a gallant, but low-cost attempt to duplicate an Italian plaza, cozy secluded booths surrounded a small fountain set on a floor of faux stones. Hanging baskets of plastic flowers provided splashes of garish color.

The four women took a booth and perused the menu. They finally decided on a vegetarian and a chicken pesto pizza. Cathy added an order of breadsticks to the order. "I know it's overkill but bread is my weakness," she said. She went to place the order and came back with a tray of soft drinks.

While they waited for their order, Max asked about their afternoon. The group had visited several gift and antique shops.

"But none of them were as cool as that quilt shop this morning," Mary said. "Thank you again for taking us out there."

"No problem," Lil replied. "I loved it myself. By the time we get home, I'll have enough projects for the whole winter. Actually, I got so excited about the choices, I forgot to ask you a couple more things about Barbara. You know that my son works for the bank that sponsors the haunted house, and they're trying to raise money for a new auditorium at the school. But they can't really reopen unless the murder is solved. So we're trying to find out what we can to help out."

"Really?" Mary said. "I love it—you're just like Nancy Drew, only a little older."

Max laughed. "Thank you for that. More like Jessica Fletcher, but still 'a little' older. We were wondering if Barbara ever showed anyone in your group a photo of this guy that she knew from Burnsville?"

A waiter brought their pizza, plates and forks.

Mary appeared in deep thought. "I don't think so."

But Cathy slapped the table and turned to Mary. "Yes, she did! We were in that wine bar at the last hotel, and you had gone to bed. That was when she told me when the cruise was and that she met this guy...she had a picture on her phone." She sat back in the booth. "It was weird. He was kind of frumpy looking and she made him sound like a dreamboat."

Max smiled, wondering when was the last time she had heard the term 'dreamboat.'

"It was a selfie and you could see the ocean in the background. It must have been windy because his hair was kind of sticking up."

"Thank you," Lil said. "That's good to know. I imagine the police have found her phone and they can check it out. You see, we have speculated that Al Carson wasn't his real name, and maybe he killed her to avoid having anyone here in town know about his romance with her."

"Oh, gosh," Cathy said. "That's awful. Do you know what the guy's name really is?"

"We might," Max said. "The police are working on it." At least, she hoped they were.

"Is there anything else Barbara said that might indicate who would murder her?" Lil asked.

"No," Mary said. "How do you know it wasn't just random?"

"We don't. But we wonder what she was doing there, or if she was killed somewhere else, why did the killer move her body to the haunted house?" Max lifted a piece of gooey pizza from the pan to her plate, swiping at the long string of cheese, and continued. "It was a deliberate attempt to stage the body, and the main customers were children, for heaven's sake. That's really sick."

"Well, Barbara certainly didn't seem worried or scared. She was really hoping to meet up with this Al Carson guy. Or whatever his name was." Cathy took a big bite of her slice. "Mmmmm. This is yummy."

Mary shivered. "Can we talk about something else? This murder spooks me out. Cathy said you sisters travel together a lot? That sounds wonderful. My sister died three years ago from heart problems, and I miss her so much. I wish we had done some traveling together."

"Do you have any other siblings?" Cathy asked.

Lil laughed. "Actually we have two younger sisters and a brother. But they all have families and our sisters think we're nuts. I'm not sure they would go with us even if they were alone." She looked at Max.

"I'm sure they wouldn't."

The rest of meal, Max and Lil recounted some of their adventures, and Mary and Cathy talked about some of the tours they had taken.

"We met a year ago on a bus trip to Kentucky," Mary said. "It followed the Bourbon Trail." She smirked at Cathy. "Cathy likes her bourbon."

"Oh, hush," Cathy said. "I didn't notice you avoiding it. One night—omigosh!"

They all swiveled their heads toward the pickup counter where Cathy was staring.

"It's Art Carnel," Max said. His back was to them but his face was easily visible in the overhead curved mirror.

"I think that's the guy in the picture with Barbara!" Cathy said in a low voice.

Just then Carnel looked up into the mirror and frowned. He paid for his pizza and turned around.

"Ladies," he said with a faint smile, nodded and walked out the door.

"Are you sure?" Lil asked Cathy.

"Well, I couldn't swear to it but it sure looks like him."

"You may have to identify a photo for the sheriff. Especially if they never found Barbara's phone," Max told her.

Mary shuddered. "Because he might be the murderer."

Max nodded. "It's possible."

They finished stuffing themselves as they rehashed the killing, in spite of Mary's unease about the subject, and asked the waiter for carryout boxes. Max and Lil didn't learn anything else new. Mary paid the bill and they headed back to the Hilltop Inn.

After exchanging email addresses and good luck wishes on their respective travels, Mary and Cathy waved goodbye, and Max and Lil left for Terry's house.

On the way, they approached the country road that led to the haunted house. Max slowed down.

Lil frowned. "What are you doing?"

"I know we can't get in the house, but I'd like to take a look around. All that rain, there should be tracks left by the murderer."

"Unless the rain washed them all away."

"I won't know unless I look."

"It's dark out."

"Of course it is. It's—" Max looked at her watch in the streetlight—"7:30 pm in October. It's always dark then."

"I don't think it's a good idea," Lil said, and gripped the door handle just in time as Max spun the wheel toward the country blacktop.

"Look at it this way—we can take a quick look around without anyone questioning where we are—Terry, Camille, the police chief…"

"Maybe if we are worried about accounting to those people, there's a good reason. They would say we are nuts! This is probably dumber than breaking in to Dutch Schultz's apartment last summer."

"Probably," Maxine said cheerfully.

Lil sighed and folded her arms, but made no further comment.

They reached the lane and Max drove carefully up to the house. The headlights only picked out the drive and the dead leaves alongside. The signs of course were still gone, and when they pulled up in front of the house, the porch was wrapped with crime scene tape.

"Hand me the flashlight out of the glovebox," Max ordered.

"Yes, Ma'am!" Lil shot back.

Max ducked under the tape and climbed the steps to try the door. Locked, as she expected. She descended the steps and headed around the side of the house. The other door opened on the Studebaker.

"Wait!" Lil called.

Max turned and used the light to guide Lil's feet as she stumbled as fast as she could through the piles of leaves and brush. "I thought you'd stay in the car."

"Not by myself."

"Oh, right," Max laughed. "Like I'm any protection."

Lil bent over to catch her breath. "But I don't want to die alone."

"That's encouraging. Okay, let's see what we can find." Max swept the flashlight back and forth ahead of them.

The shrubs and plantings along the house suffered from both overgrown weeds and early frosts. Some appeared to be beaten down by the storm and others possibly trampled. The trampled areas weren't necessarily near windows, though, so no logical explanation for them came to mind.

At the back of the house, rather than go through the garden, Max turned away from the house and walked along the garden fence. At the corner, a barely discernible path led into the woods. Max followed it.

"Are you sure this is a good idea?" Lil whispered.

"Of course not. But I think there are some outbuildings down this way. I saw them from an upstairs window the first day we came here."

"Don't you think the police have checked this all out?"

"Maybe. But maybe not."

Lil scoffed. "You wouldn't admit it even if you had watched them do it."

"Maybe not."

"This is stupid."

"Jeez-Louise, Lil, what did you come along tonight for?"

"A free pizza. Why are you stopping?"

"Because of this fence across the path." Max stepped to the side and aimed the flashlight at a barricade ahead.

Lil moved around her and peered past the fence into the darkness. "It's another farm or something, you think?

Looks like the woods end. I can tell there are large buildings around an open lot."

"I can't see if there's a house or not, but it doesn't feel abandoned. Let's go back. This doesn't feel right." Max led the way back up the path.

"It never did feel right," Lil muttered.

When they reached the garden fence, they skirted it toward the back of the lot. The unearthly ballroom dancers swayed in the breeze, barely visible in the ambient light.

Max remembered a tool shed and perhaps another building behind that on the other side of the garden. They walked between the garden fence and more overgrown woods. The normal night sounds seemed amplified—an owl hooting in the distance, scrabbling noises in the underbrush, and distant traffic noises from the nearest highway. A twig broke.

Lil grabbed Max by the shoulder. "What was that?"

"Just an animal. Relax."

Lil listened harder and tried to walk more quietly. She thought she heard a cough. Her ears playing tricks maybe.

Maybe not.

They reached the tool shed.

"Here, hold the flashlight." Max turned the simple chunk of wood nailed to the doorframe and pulled the door open. "Shine it in here."

Lil made none of her usual comments on Max's bossiness and pointed the light toward the interior of the

109

shed. The usual rakes, shovels, and spades stood along the walls. A rusted push mower took up most of the center and a few chipped clay pots lined the high shelves.

"What is that in the corner?'

Lil gasped as she illuminated the pile of cloth and recognized an arm poking out to one side.

Max answered her own question. "I think it's a manikin." She took the light and maneuvered around the mower.

"The one that was in the bedroom?"

Max pulled the lumpy object, like a large rag doll, upright. It had no clothes or hair but sported dark eye makeup and bright garish lips.

"I don't think so. It didn't have this kind of makeup. This one—or one like it—was at the dining room table. It reminded me of Morticia Addams."

"Who?"

"You know—the *Addams Family*. My favorite TV show back in the day."

"Oh, ick." Lil shuddered. "I hated that show."

"Yeah, well. There's the difference between us."

"I wondered why they replaced this manikin. Doesn't look like there's anything wrong with it," Lil said.

"Unless..." Max said. "Nobody from the crew went into the dining room the night of the murder, did they?"

Lil looked around the rest of the shed. A high shelf to the left of the door held containers of chemicals, clay pots, and a bag of potting soil. "Terry shined his light in there but it looked like there wasn't any disturbance."

She lifted a tattered jacket off a hook below the shelf. Underneath, a long-handled lopper and a ring of old keys hung on the same hook. A coiled extension cord hung on the next hook and an old apron on the next.

"And we went through the dining room later to get the lanterns. but I didn't look around," Max continued. She noticed a pair of rubber boots and galvanized bucket sitting below the hooks. There didn't seem to be much else in the shed.

"I didn't either."

"So when we left, the police were there, but the house hasn't been left unlocked since. No coming and going except the investigators, correct?"

Lil looked at her sister, puzzled. "What are you saying?"

"Maybe the killer hid the manikin from the bedroom in plain sight. None of the people who know what's supposed to be where have been back in there. Let's go do some window-peeping." She led the way out of the shed, leaving Lil to close up the shed in the dark.

"Dammit, Max, wait up!"

She did so reluctantly, and they returned to the side of the house. "These would be in the dining room, right?" She pointed at a pair of long windows in the middle of the side wall, two dark rectangles, barely distinguishable from the only slightly lighter siding, once white but now a weathered gray.

"Should be," Lil said. "Actually, maybe someone could have gotten into the house. There was a ring of keys hanging in the shed under that old jacket." Max didn't answer.

Lil followed her through the weeds, cringing as she felt burrs sticking to her good slacks. Max stood on her toes and aimed the flashlight in one of the windows. The dusty velvet drapes were tied back with heavy gold cords but the sheers behind them still made visibility difficult.

"I can't tell for sure." Max strained with the effort of standing on her toes and holding the flashlight over her head. "I think there's one maybe that has blood on the face. They must have redressed it and used the wig from the one in the tool shed. But it's facing away from the door and toward the windows so we wouldn't have noticed it from inside."

A gruff male voice came from behind them. "Aren't you the clever old biddy?"

Max yelped, dropped the flashlight, and ran along the house. Lil screamed and tried to follow but strong hands grabbed her arms.

CHAPTER ELEVEN
MAX

MAX CRAWLED BEHIND a brambly bush and peered back at the spot she had left. Her flashlight was half buried in the leaves and pointed toward the back of the house. The obstructed beam was no help. She could hear Lil whimpering and scuffling. Without thinking beyond the next moment, she heaved herself to her feet, wincing at the pain in her knees, and charged toward the sounds.

She crashed into the bodies.

"Lil! Grab my hand!" Fumbling in the dark, she was able to see Lil's pale hand close to her face and clutched it. At the same time, she stiff-armed the dark shape behind Lil. She and her sister started tumbling back.

"Hey!" the voice yelled. Max just managed to stay upright and pulled Lil toward what she thought was the front of the house and her car. As they got close, a flashlight wielded by their pursuer lit up the red Studebaker ahead of them. It stood out against the dead trees like a beacon.

Max searched her coat pocket for her keys. No luck. Fear clutched at her heart. As she found the keys in her other pocket, she noticed the driver's side front tire was flat and totally slashed to shreds.

Lil's voice shook behind her: "He's coming, Max!"

"We aren't going to get out with the car," Max growled. "Follow me." She took off around the other side of the house, but listened to make sure her sister was still behind her.

On the opposite of the house, Max headed for a large rectangular shape along the side of the house. She felt around in the middle, grabbed a handle, and jerked the wooden basement door open.

"Quick!" She said to Lil. "Down the steps."

The man's voice yelled again. "Hey!" Max didn't think he had rounded the corner of the house yet. Max followed Lil down into the black hole. Both of them slipped and stumbled down the rickety wood stairs. Max was suddenly blinded by the smallest of flames. Lil held a cigarette lighter up so Max could see to reach up and close the door.

Once that was done, Max turned on her sister. "I thought you quit," she hissed.

"I did. But I'm not going to throw out a perfectly good lighter." She flicked the lighter again and pointed at the side of the door. "There's a bar there that goes through those brackets. If we put that in, he won't be able to get the doors open. Here hold this." She thrust the lighter at Max. "I'll do it. Just hold that still."

She grabbed the bar at the side and worked it through the brackets just as they heard their pursuer pounding on the door.

The two women ducked into the basement and realized there was another door, standing open, at the bottom of the steps. Lil pushed it shut. Max searched the area with the lighter held high and spotted an old dresser.

"Quick, help me drag this over in front of the door."

The uneven brick and dirt floor made pushing much harder, but they managed to get the door at least partially blocked.

"Do you have your phone?" Max asked. "I left mine in my purse in the car. So stupid!"

Lil felt her jacket pockets. "I do!" She pulled it out.

"Call 911. And then we can use it for a flashlight."

Lil dialed. The basement echoed with a wrenching screech. An axe blade split the door above the dresser. Just barely but enough for the edge of the blade to glimmer in the dim light.

"C'mon! We need to find the stairs!" Max grabbed the phone from Lil and aimed it toward the back of the basement. "Gotta be back here—I think the stairs are off the kitchen."

A voice from the phone saying, "What is your emergency?" was punctuated with another hit to the door.

The light from the phone revealed rickety wooden steps toward the back. As they stumbled toward the stairs, Max gave the 911 operator their situation and location. "Help please! We're at the—Kell house, on Cranberry Road and being chased!"

"Chased?"

"Yes, by a man with an axe!" She shoved the phone in her pocket.

Lil whispered, "He's stopped pounding."

They climbed the steps, Max first, both of them panting. Three steps from the top, noises on the other side of the door brought Max to a halt.

"He's in the house! Quick back down!"

But Lil wasn't fast enough for her sister. In her fear, Max tried to go around her, and when she put her weight on the same step, the wood cracked deafeningly. They tumbled and screamed. Max grabbed the handrail, but Lil plummeted to the bottom.

"Ohmigod, Lil—I'm so sorry—" Using the rail, she hurried down to the heap at the bottom.

Max got down on her knees, ignoring the shooting pain from her arthritis, and shined the phone toward Lil's face. Her eyes were closed and she breathed in rasps.

"What have I done? Lil—Lil! Sweetie, speak to me."

"Sweetie?" Lil croaked. "You've lost it. Ohh, my leg!"

Max glanced up the steps but couldn't hear or see anything. Did their pursuer leave?

"We need to hide. Maybe behind the furnace. I know it hurts but we have to hide somewhere if we want to stay alive." Using the light on the phone again, she looked around the basement. Near the furnace a few pieces of coal laid scattered on the floor by an old coal chute and under the chute—a wheelbarrow!

She hobbled over to drag the wheelbarrow back. "I'm going to try and get you in here, okay?" She didn't wait for an answer but pulled Lil's left arm over her shoulders and gently as she could, lifted her toward the wheelbarrow. The injured leg was partially supported by the sloping front of the barrow.

Lil gripped the sides, but let go to wipe some of the tears streaming down her face. In the dim light of the phone, Max could see streaks across Lil's face from the coal dust. Best not to mention that.

"It must be broken," Lil sobbed.

Max grimaced. "I wouldn't make you do this if the alternative wasn't so much worse. Can you hold the phone? Literally."

"Funny," Lil gasped and took the phone in her right hand. She aimed the light in the general direction of the furnace but was unable to hold it very steady. Their progress was slow and wobbly, accompanied by grunts and groans. Something brushed Max's face. She shrieked and almost dropped the wheelbarrow handle.

"What is it?" Lil whispered.

"Spider webs."

"I don't know how…someone as tough as you…can be so scared of spiders," Lil said between clenched teeth. "Do you hear that guy?"

"No. Not since we came back down the steps. Hold the light up."

All the while, Max listened for any sounds from upstairs but didn't hear any. When they finally were obscured by the furnace from either of the entrances, Max lowered the wheelbarrow gently.

"Yeow!" Lil cried. Apparently not gently enough. Then for a few moments, the only sound was their own heavy breathing.

Max stood up. She took the phone and used it to look around. "I guess this didn't gain us much. We're not very well hidden."

"Help should be here soon, right?" Lil's voice was getting weak.

"Sure," Max said with more confidence than she felt. Lil began to shake. "I'm freezing."

"Here—it's not much but might help some." Max struggled out of her fleece jacket and tucked it around Lil.

A door opened above them. Max switched off the light on the phone. Heavy footsteps sounded as well as some other unidentifiable sounds. Someone began to pry the basement door open.

Max held her breath as she tried to determine how she would know if it was friend or foe.

A voice from the top of the wrecked stairs called, "Hello?"

Before they could reply, loud crashes came from the step area and a furry freight train barreled into Max.

"Rosie!"

"Mom? Aunt Max?" Terry's voice called again. "What happened to the steps?"

Max used the phone light again to find her way back into the other room. "We had a little accident. There's an outside stairway." She pointed to that side of the house. "But we barricaded it."

Terry bent over and peered toward where she pointed. "Can you pull that chest away? I'll send the police around that way." He started to straighten up and then said, "Where's Mother?"

"Back behind the furnace." Max paused. "She may have a broken leg."

"What—? Never mind. We'll get her out of there as soon as we can."He raised his voice. "Help is coming, Mom!" He left.

Max tried to move the dresser out far enough to get the door open. Rosie alternated between dancing around her mistress with joy and sniffing out the wonderfully intriguing corners of the basement. Max heard no sound from Lil.

When she got the door open, she could see the destruction of the bulkhead doors their assailant had wreaked with the axe. Boards had been chopped out leaving only the frame.Two police officers pulled broken boards away to clear the steps. One paused and looked down at Max. "This guy was serious."

Max gulped. "Yes, he was. Did you catch him?"

"There was no one around when we got here."

She moved back and tugged more on the dresser but gave up and returned to check on Lil. Her sister was barely conscious.

"They're almost here, Lil. Hold on, sweetie."

The sound of the dresser crashing to its side signaled the police breaching of the entrance. Terry was right behind them.

"Max? Mom?"

"In here," Max called back. Flashlight beams bounced off the dirty stone walls as the police led Terry to the furnace room. Max felt doubly guilty for getting her sister into this when she saw the worry on Terry's face.

EMTs arrived and carried Lil out on a stretcher. As they loaded her, Max caught a glimpse of black coal dust smeared all over the back of Lil's clothes. Another strike against her. Terry ran alongside holding his mother's hand.

The police chief arranged to have Max's car towed to a tire shop in town. He helped her back out the bulkhead stairs, around the house to the back door and into the kitchen. Rosie stayed right at her heels. In spite of the lack of heat, the protection from the wind made the house warmer than the outside.

Mansell pulled out a chair at the table and helped Max sit.

"I want to go to the hospital with my sister."

"Can you tell me what happened? Then I'll give you a ride to the clinic."

Max told her story in fits and starts, keeping her eyes down so she didn't have to see the disbelief and accusation on his face.

"What possessed you to come here by yourselves at night?"

Max shrugged. "Just thought we'd take a look around. We did find some clues."

"Really?" Mansell's voice dripped with sarcasm. "And what would those clues be?"

"Well, a clue I should say. There's a manikin in a shed out back that I think used to be at the dining room table. I think the one in the dining room with the blood on its face is the one that was in the bedroom."

Mansell got up, smacked the swinging door with one hand, and walked into the dining room. He was back in a moment.

"I see what you mean. But what's the significance? What kind of 'clue' is that?"

"I don't know. But the murderer went to a lot of work to stage a scene. What was he trying to accomplish?"

"Let's work at this from a more concrete angle instead of your 'pie in the sky' ideas. Who was chasing you? Did you recognize a voice? What did he say?"

Max tried to reconstruct events after they found the manikin in the shed. "When he came up behind us, he said something like 'Pretty smart for an old biddy.' I know he called us old biddies. Then he yelled 'Hey!' — twice, I think — when he was chasing us. I think that's all we heard him say. And we don't know that many people around here so I don't know how we could identify him from that." She paused. "Although his voice did sound a little familiar."

121

"Think! Who have you met while you were here?"

"Hmmm. Art Carnel. But I don't think it was his voice. Oh—I forgot to tell you! We had pizza with two of the women from the bus tour tonight. While we were eating, Art came in and one of the women said she was sure it was the same guy who Barbara had shown her a photo of—Al Carson."

"That doesn't mean he's the murderer, but we'll check it out. Who else have you met?"

"Of course, quite a few men came through the haunted house, but I don't know that I would remember any of their voices. A couple of the volunteers. There's a guy named Bert who works at the bank with Terry and a science teacher—Vince something? I can't think of any other men that we've actually visited with. Oh, the guy that owns the Inn—Wendell—and a couple of men on the bus tour."

Mansell folded his arms. "Let's head in to the clinic. We can continue this discussion on the way."

Max stood. "What about my dog?"

"She won't be the first dog to ride in that cruiser. I don't know if I can lock the house. Terry had a key and I forgot to have him leave it. Maybe there's a deadbolt I can lock before we go out."

Max snapped her fingers. "Lil said she saw a ring of keys in the shed under a jacket. She wondered if that's how the murderer got in to the house."

"Let's go. We'll check it out quick before we leave."

Max led him through the garden to the tool shed. She shivered with the evening chill and the lack of her jacket. It would be just her luck to come down with pneumonia. Or maybe she deserved it for dragging Lil into this. The thought of Lil's severe pain made Max's stomach clench.

Mansell opened the shed and shone the light around.

"There's the old jacket." Max pointed to the row of hooks.

Chief Mansell lifted the jacket. He pulled on a pair of latex gloves and picked up the ring of keys. "Some of these look old enough to be the keys to the house." They headed back to the house, while he examined the keys with the flashlight. He separated out a couple and stumbled twice. When they got to the back door, he tried them both and the second one worked.

"Okay." He aimed the flashlight at the steps and the ground beyond. "We'll have to go around the side. My cruiser's out front."

They passed the crippled Studebaker on their way. "The tow truck should be here any time. I'll check with them when we get to town."

Max nodded, but her feelings of guilt threatened to lay her out flat. If she hadn't followed her wild hair idea, neither her sister nor her car would be lame.

123

CHAPTER TWELVE
MAX

CHIEF MANSELL SEEMED to run out of questions, and they rode in silence in to town. He placed the ring of keys in an evidence bag on the console between them, and Max picked them up to look at them in the light of the passing streetlights.

"One of these keys is very different," she commented, holding up a small brass key. "It looks a lot newer." The old *Sesame Street* ditty, "One of these things is not like the others," started to run through her head.

"I noticed that," Mansell said, without looking.

"Kind of looks like a safe deposit key."

Mansell nodded.

Max turned toward him. "I know you probably can't talk about it to me, but this whole thing makes no sense. Why put the body on display? The only reason I can think of is exactly what happened: shut down the haunted house and keep people away from it."

"It didn't keep you away from it."

"And that made somebody pretty unhappy. That nun's habit makes it seem like there's a connection between the murder and that old robbery. Could the money have been hidden here? But why would they have left it that long?"

Mansell pulled into the parking lot of a small clinic. He put the cruiser in park and turned to her.

"We got confirmation today that fingerprints found on a cross that was with the habit belonged to a man who died in prison. He was arrested for another crime shortly after the robbery here."

"But there's still one robber at large as far as you know."

"All the more reason for you to be cautious and stay away from that house. I see Terry's car here so I assume you will get a ride with him. I'll take your dog to his house and check back later to see how your sister is doing."

As the chief pulled away, Max felt a mix of humiliation and guilt.

INSIDE THE CLINIC, a brightly-lit. waiting room greeted Max. One young couple sat holding hands, worried frowns on their faces. While Max stood at the counter, a nurse came out and called "Mr. and Mrs. Hurd?" The couple jumped up to follow her back down a hallway.

A young man at the desk turned from his computer. "Can I help you?"

"My sister, Lillian Garrett, was brought in by ambulance?"

"Yes, she's in that first cubicle to the right." He pointed down another hall where several divided sections were enclosed by curtains.

Max walked to the first curtain and pulled it aside tentatively. Lil lay on a table with Terry by her side. The right leg of her pants had been cut open and a middle-aged woman in a white coat was examining the leg. Black coal dust smeared the pristine white examining table.

"Come in." Lil gave her a weak smile and spoke in a thin, raspy voice. "Some of your investigating is kind of hard on my wardrobe."

Terry turned to look at Max and frowned. He did not take this as lightly as his mother.

Max walked up to them. "I'm so sorry. It was a stupid thing to do."

"Yes, it was," Terry said. His voice was flat.

In spite of knowing her culpability, Max was taken aback. Terry had never been less than respectful to her. She stood there a few moments, unsure of what to say. Terry turned back to his mother.

Finally she asked, "Is it broken?"

"I'm afraid so," answered the doctor. "A small fracture. I'm going to try splinting it first. At her age, we don't have to worry about too much activity."

Terry rolled his eyes. "I wish."

Max said, "I think I should go to the waiting room." She left.

MAX TRIED LOOKING at a magazine but couldn't concentrate. She found the restroom, washed her face ,and smoothed her hair. Her socks were covered with burrs and her jacket pocket was ripped. After she had done what she could to restore her appearance, she returned to the waiting room.

She sat and stared into space. The only other person in the waiting room was the young man at the desk. Her brain went from regrets over her part in Lil's injuries to puzzling over the identity of their attacker and back again.

Finally, Terry came out of the cubicle, pulling on his jacket. "They're going to keep her overnight. Let's get home." He didn't wait for an answer but headed for the door. However, his upbringing would not allow him to ignore his manners, and he stopped to hold the door for his aunt.

Once in the car, Max asked, "Did the doctor splint it or did she have to use a cast?"

"There's a splint on it for now," Terry said.

"Does Melody know what happened?"

"Of course. I've been talking to her." Nothing more was said until they pulled in the driveway. He turned to Max. "I'll handle the kids' questions. I don't want you alarming them about their grandmother."

Max felt insulted and hurt. "Of course I wouldn't."

He raised his eyebrows at her, shut off the car and got out. Once again he held the front door and inside, took her coat.

Max's antics were beginning to exact a price on her joints and muscles, and she hobbled to the kitchen. Melody and the kids were at the table playing a game of Chutes and Ladders.

127

"Aunt Max!" Ren said. "Rosie came home in the police car! Where have you been? Where's Granny Lil?"

"Your dad will tell you all about it." She turned to Melody. "Do you have any coffee made, by any chance?"

Melody started to get up. "I can make some—unless you'd rather have a glass of wine."

"Sit still. That does sound good, but I'll get it."

"There's an open bottle of Chardonnay in the fridge."

Max poured a glass and sat down away from the table while they finished their game.

Rival turned in his chair. "Dad! What happened to Granny Lil?"

"She broke a bone in her leg and they had to put a splint on it. Remember when Ren had to have a splint on her arm? Granny'll stay at the clinic tonight and we'll pick her up in the morning."

"How did she break her leg?" Ren asked.

"She fell. Now pick up your game because it's time for you to get up to bed."

REN AND RIVAL raced each other to put pieces in the box, and then charged up the steps. Melody poured herself a glass of wine and sat back down at the table. She grinned at Max. "So spill! What were you two up to?"

Terry sat down with a bottle of beer. "Mel, it isn't funny,"

"Of course the broken leg isn't, but the rest sounds pretty exciting." She turned back to Max. "So do tell."

Max related an abbreviated version of events. When she got to the part about the assailant trying to break down the door with an axe, Melody's eyes got wide.

"Wow! Weren't you scared?"

"Very," Max said. "That's when we tried to get up the stairs to get out through the house. But he beat us there and barricaded the door. When we tried to get back down the stairs, one of the steps broke and that's when Lil got hurt." She paused and took a sip of her wine. "Fortunately we were able to call 911, and the sirens must have scared him off. We did discover a couple of important things before that all happened, though." She told them about the manikin and the ring of keys.

Terry, who had been looking as disgusted as possible, seemed to grow more interested in spite of himself. "The missing manikin was at the dining room table?"

Max nodded. "And the one that had been at the table was in the tool shed. The keys looked like they were all for the house, except for one that Chief Mansell and I thought looked like a safe deposit box key."

"The bank can check that and at least see if it's from our bank." Terry seemed to have forgotten that he was mad at Max.

Max finished her glass of wine and rinsed the glass out at the sink. "I know it's not terribly late, but I believe I'm done."

"I should think," Melody said. "And the kids took Rosie out in the yard for a while after the chief brought her home."

129

Max looked at the dog lying across the doorway, snoring peacefully. She went over and nudged the dog gently with her toe. "C'mon, girl. It's time we both turned in."

MAX BARELY REMEMBERED her head hitting the pillow, and was deep in slumber when her phone rang a couple of hours later.

She tried to figure out where she was and when. "Hello?"

"Max! It's Lil!"

Max sat up. "What's wrong?"

"Nothing. But I think I know who that voice was — you know — the guy who attacked us."

It took a moment but then clicked. "Who?"

"The guy from the Inn — that creepy Wendell."

Max yawned and considered. "I dunno. He's a creep but he kind of passive. I can't imagine him swinging that axe. And what would be his motive?"

Lil sighed. "No idea."

"How are you doing?"

"Okay. I slept for a while, but now I've been laying here awake and got to thinking about that voice. Guess I'll turn the TV on for a while."

"Your son is really mad at me," Max said.

"That's silly. I should have just stayed in the car. As you suggested."

"Then he just would have attacked you there. No, I never should have turned down that road. So stupid. The

Chief will probably be in to see you in the morning. If not, we'll contact him with your idea."

"I think Terry's going to pick me up early."

"Good. I'll see you then. Sleep well."

CHAPTER THIRTEEN
MAX

WEDNESDAY MORNING DAWNED OVERCAST, but warm. Max dragged herself out of bed, sore in every muscle and extremity. Rosie cocked her head and watched her mistress struggle with her robe and slippers.

"It'll be a few minutes, girl," Max told her. "In dog years, I'm over five hundred years old and I feel every bit of it."

She shuffled to the bathroom and when she came out, searched her suitcase for her most comfortable clothes. The navy blue sweats that she pulled out weren't glamorous, but then neither was she. Rosie followed her every move, eternally hopeful that the next one would lead outside.

Finally Max got the leash and took the dog out the back door. They walked around the side of the house and took the sidewalk to the little bridge. By the time they returned, the smell of coffee called her to the kitchen.

Terry sat at the table reading the paper. He looked up and nodded. His face looked a little less angry than it had the night before.

"Mom just called and the doctor won't be releasing her until about 10:00. I'm going to go into work, but I will stop and get a wheelchair from the American Legion before I pick her up. They have them to borrow."

Melody set a mug of coffee in front of Max. "The tire shop called a little bit ago and they already have the tire replaced. You can pick the car up when it's convenient." She stopped and grinned. "I think he wants to keep it a little longer."

Terry said, "I can drop you off there on my way to work if you want."

Max sat down. "I would appreciate that. I really would. Listen, Terry, I'm so sorry —"

He waved her off. "I was upset last night. I know no one can keep you two in line." He grinned at her. "I try to remember that it's better than having Mom vegetating in a home somewhere."

Max smiled back. "Maybe. I hope so. Do you think she'll need to be in a wheel chair for long?"

Terry scoffed. "Hopefully at least until I get her in the car. Then probably crutches or a walker for a while."

"I'll go put on something a little more presentable and then I'll be ready to go."

As she was getting dressed, her cell phone rang.

"Max? I'm so glad I caught you. This is Mary Carmody. I think I left my purse in your car — on the floor in the back. Did you find it?"

"Uh, no. But I got a flat tire and had to have it towed to the shop in town." She didn't think it was the time to

133

go into the whole sordid story. "I'm going to pick it up in just a bit. I'm sure the purse is probably still there, but I'll call you as soon as I get to the tire place. When does your bus leave?"

"About noon. Oh, I hope it's there—my cards, ID, everything is in it! It's red leather."

"I understand. I'll call you in the next hour and bring your purse out after I get the car, okay?"

"Thank you! I will really owe you now! I'd forget my head if it wasn't attached."

THE TIRE SHOP was a typical small town business, with a couple of older guys drinking coffee in the waiting room. They bantered with the owner and laughed at their private jokes. They appeared to be just passing the time rather than paying customers.

When Max walked up to the counter, the owner looked her over and said "The Studebaker?"

"Yes. Terry said you have it done already?"

"I do. Here's the good news." He laid the bill in front of her.

"Do you know if there was a purse left in the back?"

The owner shrugged. "I was only in the front. If it was there, it should still be there."

One of the two guys behind her said, "Sweet car!"

She turned. "Thank you. I like it." She paid the bill, and while she waited for the owner to bring it around to the front, the men questioned her about where she got it and the restoration process.

The owner pulled the car up in front. He came in and handed her the keys and a red leather purse. "Is this it?"

"Yes. Thank you. A friend left it there last night. I need to drop it off at the Hilltop Inn. Can you tell me how to get there from here?"

"Sure. Go right when you leave here and turn left on Barr Street—about two blocks down. That will take you back to the highway. Go right and follow it out of town. The Inn will be on your left."

One of the old guys spoke up. "Don't let old Wendell get you!" They both laughed.

Max said, "He doesn't seem like much of a threat."

"Don't let his looks fool you. He works out regularly. Thinks he's a real Cassanova. Or Mr. World." They were still laughing as she walked out the door.

As SHE DROVE toward the Inn, Max mulled over their information. If Wendell Welter was stronger than he looked, he could have easily been their attacker. The big question was still motive, but combined with Lil's identification of his voice, it sounded like he had the means.

As she passed a sign for the downtown business district, she looked at her watch. She had time. She made a snap decision and turned. Terry might not know much about Welter, but Camille should.

Max pulled into the bank parking lot and hurried inside. Terry was busy, so she just waved and asked Camille's secretary if she was available. In a few minutes, the secretary returned and ushered her into Camille's office.

Camille turned and stood from her computer and indicated one of the customer chairs.

"Max! Terry was just telling me this morning about your experience last night. How scary! And your sister has a broken leg? Do you know yet who did it?" She set a mug of coffee in front of Max.

Max shook her head. "We don't know for sure who it was, but we have some ideas. I was just headed out to the Inn, but first I have some questions." She paused and took a breath. "How well do you know Wendell Welter?"

Camille sat down at her desk. "Wendell? What on earth—?"

"Bear with me a moment. Has he always lived here?"

"As far as I know. He worked for a cleaning service for years—as a matter of fact, the one that cleaned the bank. Then about four or five years ago, he got a small inheritance. The Inn was for sale at the time, and he used the money to make the down payment."

"How successful is the Inn?"

Camille tapped a pencil on her desk. "Oh...I think he's doing okay. It hasn't made him wealthy, but summer and fall seem to be the busy times. And I think he likes what he does. But tell me why you think he is connected to all of this?"

Max sat back in her chair. "Lil thinks she recognized his voice last night. And a couple of the guys at the tire shop this morning said he works out a lot—like he might be pretty strong."

Camille looked skeptical. "But why would he do that? Any of it?"

"You just gave me an idea. You said he bought the Inn four or five years ago when he came into some money?"

"Yes."

"And the bank robbery was about five years ago?"

"Yesss, it was." Camille cocked her head to one side and studied Max.

"There were two robbers. The chief said yesterday that one died in prison for a different crime—they found fingerprints on a cross with that nun's habit, but—"

"But the other robber was never caught." Camille finished the thought.

"The only reason we've been able to come up with for the murderer displaying Barbara Gunter's body that way is to frighten people away from the house. I think there must be something hidden at that house connected with the robbery."

Camille nodded. "What about Art? You seemed certain he had something to do with all of this." She began tapping the pencil more forcefully.

"I'm sorry, Camille, but I think he is connected, although not intentionally. Wendell said the other day that he overheard a woman on the phone arranging to meet someone at the Kell house the day of murder. Barbara was the only tour member there at the time."

"But Art—"

"One of the women on the tour recognized Art from a photo Barbara had shown her of 'Al Carson.' I think she was going to meet Art at the house, but Wendell caught up with her first. Or later, I don't know."

Camille took a deep breath and picked up her desk phone. "I need to get this straightened out once and for all. If Art is a sleaze, like you say, I want to know, so I can be done with him. If he's not, I want to quit looking at him for signs of guilt all the time."

"Who are you calling?"

"Chief Mansell. You should not go anywhere near Wendell Welter until we know what's going on."

The Chief arrived in less than ten minutes. When he saw Max sitting in Camille's office, he frowned and shook his head. "I thought I made it clear that you needed to stay out of this."

"You told me to stay away from the Kell house. I have."

He shook his head again and sat in the other customer chair. Camille and Max filled him in on their guesses as to the robbery and the murder.

"I think you may have something there," he said grudgingly. "It makes as much sense as anything else we've come up with." He held up the plastic bag with the ring of keys. "Camille, can you tell me if the brass key in here came from your bank?"

She reached across the deck and picked it up. "It certainly looks like one of ours." She turned to her computer and typed in some numbers and letters, looking closely at the key as she did so.

"I'll tell you now that the only fingerprints on it belong to one of the robbers—Bernie Godwink, the one who died in prison," Mansell said.

"So, we'll assume the lessor of the box is deceased. According to our records, that person is Rudolf Stutman. Hmmm. He died in 1975."

Chief Mansell squinted at Camille. "Sooo…"

"So this Bernie must have used a stolen ID and Social Security number to get the lockbox."

Mansell picked up the bag of keys. "The mud is clearing a little. We'll talk more later." He left, nearly running over Terry who was standing right outside the door.

He walked into the office. "What's that about?"

Max filled him in as quickly as she could. "I need to go out to the Hilltop to drop off Mary's purse. Their tour group is leaving by noon. Could you go with me?"

Terry looked at Camille. "Is that okay, boss?"

Camille grabbed a sweater off the back of her chair. "Only if you take me, too. Besides," she said to Max, "you promised me a ride in that car."

Terry wanted Camille to ride in the front seat, but she pointed out that his knees would be at his ears if he rode in back.

Once in the car, Terry took out his phone. "I'd better call Mother and tell her I'm going to be a little late picking her up."

Chapter Fourteen
Max

THE CIRCULAR DRIVE in front of the Hilltop Inn was filled with three police cruisers, light bars flashing. Max parked the Studebaker in a side parking lot, and they cautiously trooped to the front door. It stood open so they entered. One patrolman stood in the entry. He recognized Terry and Camille.

"Can I help you, Ms. Bamford?"

"My friend has a purse that belongs to someone in the tour group that's staying here."

"They are all in the living room to the left there." He nodded toward the door. "The Chief is carrying out an interrogation in the kitchen and the bus isn't allowed to leave until he's done."

"Thank you." Camille opened the big double doors.

Mary Carmody sat on the bench by the baby grand piano. She jumped up when she spotted them. "You found it!"

Max handed her the purse. Cathy joined them.

"Thank you so much," Mary said. "We don't know what's going on, but the police are here. Did they find out who murdered Barbara?"

"They might be about to make an arrest. Mary, Cathy, this is Lil's son, Terry, and his boss, Camille Bamford."

Cathy looked around. "Where's Lil?"

Terry spotted a game table in the corner of the room surrounded by chairs. A chess set sat at the ready in the center of the table, but no one was using it. "Let's go sit over there. This may take a while."

Mary and Cathy followed them to the corner, puzzled looks on their faces. Once they were seated, Max gave a condensed version of the events after she dropped Cathy and Mary off the night before.

Both women sat with their mouths open.

"Lil has a broken leg?" Mary asked.

"Somebody chased you with an axe?" Cathy squeaked, garnering numerous looks from around the room.

Max waved her hands, trying to calm them. She noticed several in the large room who had stopped talking and edged closer to their group.

Mary and Cathy got the message, and Cathy leaned forward and lowered her voice. "So, was it the murderer, do you know?"

"Probably, but that's all we can say. So, your tour — you're headed to Lancaster next?"

"Yeah, we have quite a few tours scheduled there," Mary said.

Cathy added, "One day we're going to the Renaissance Fair nearby."

"I've been there," Camille said. "It's excellent. You'll enjoy it."

Mary was about to reply when the hallway doors opened and Chief Mansell entered. Behind him, Max could see Wendell Welter, struggling, complaining loudly, and in handcuffs, being ushered through the entry hall.

"Mr. Welter?" Cathy whispered. "He's the murderer?"

Max nodded. "We think so."

Welter shouted something about 'old biddies.'

"I'm sure he is," she added.

CHAPTER FIFTEEN

MAX

THE NEXT DAY, Max made a grocery run. Melody wasn't a complainer but the effect of the stressful week was evident in her stamina and posture. Lil was confined to the chaise lounge unless she used the walker. So armed with a list and reusable shopping bags, Max headed for the nearest supermarket.

She planned to cook a beef stew and corn bread for their supper. She selected onions, carrots and mushrooms in the produce department and then headed to the meat counter. While she waited for her order, she heard a familiar voice behind her.

"Well, if isn't the new town busybody."

She turned to see Art Carnel standing too close behind her. He kept his voice low so he wouldn't be overheard. She turned back to the counter, determined to ignore him.

But he wasn't giving up. "Unfortunately, Camille chose to believe your gossip. But it was over with Barbara before she ever came here."

Max took the package of stew meat from the butcher and turned back to Art.

"And what about the redhead at the apple fair?" She left him standing there.

THREE NIGHTS LATER, Max held the door for Lil as she shuffled through with her walker. They followed Terry and Melody through the main dining room of the Brat House to a small private room.

Rival and Ren led the procession, announcing, "We're here," to the room's occupants.

Camille Bamford was there and Josh Mansell, with his family. Josh introduced them to his wife, Alicia Mansell, and daughters, Rose and Delilah. They were the girls who originally found the nun's habit in the old house.

Mansell and Camille had invited them to a celebration dinner. Wendell Welter had confessed to the murder of Barbara Gunter and participating in the bank robbery five years previous.

Once everyone had a beverage, Mansell raised his glass of pinot noir, and said "While I don't condone your interference with the case," and he paused to look pointedly at Max and Lil, "I do admit that your insights and prodding helped to solve the case. Thank you." He tipped his head at them.

They clinked glasses.

"You promised you would fill in the holes for us," Max reminded him.

Melody held up a hand. "Let me get the kids settled." She found a box on a sideboard with puzzles and games.

The four children dove into the box, already bickering over who got what, and lost all interest in the adult conversation.

"Okay," Josh said. "As you guessed, Wendell's 'inheritance' was his half of the take from the bank robbery. He had a good opportunity to plan the robbery during those times he cleaned the bank at night."

Max asked, "How did Wendell and Bernie know each other?"

"Wendell said he met Bernie at a fast food joint where he worked at over in Baseburg-about fifteen miles from here. They visited whenever Wendell ate there. When Bernie found out about Wendell's job, he started joking about a bank heist. Eventually the joke got serious."

Camille nodded. "Wendell saw an opportunity to change his life, when the Hilltop went up for sale--if he just had a down payment."

"Exactly," Josh agreed. "Wendell was the person in the nun's habit, and Bernie Godwink drove the getaway car. Afterwards, they split the money, and Bernie offered to dispose of the nun's habit. That was the last Wendell saw of him."

"So Bernie's print got on the cross when he hid the habit," Max said.

"And he hid his half of the money in a lock box in the very bank they had robbed?" Lil asked.

"He did." Josh smiled. "Under the name, Rudolf Stutman. Crazy isn't it? He could use the ID information for a dead man because the rules for lockboxes aren't terribly stringent. The individual doesn't get any income from them, so the Feds aren't much interested."

"How did you get into the box?" Max asked.

"We were able to get a court order to open the box — the key was on that ring in the tool shed. It contained exactly half of the take from the robbery. So we surmise that shortly after the robbery, Bernie rented the lockbox. No one here knew him so he could use whatever name he wanted, as long as he had fake ID. Then he hid the key and the habit at the old Kell house."

Terry chuckled. "He obviously didn't bank on getting arrested for something else before he got back there."

"Bank on. Good one." Josh grinned. " I'm sure he planned to return fairly soon, in case the house was sold. Getting arrested for a convenience store holdup from a couple of years earlier was not part of his plan. He never got out of jail on bail, was convicted, and, as you know, died in prison."

"So what got Wendell interested in the Kell house?" Terry asked.

Max set down her wine glass. "I think you did." She smiled. "Didn't you mention the nun's habit when you were explaining the history of the house to the tour group?"

"Yeah, I guess I did. But Wendell wasn't there."

"No, but Mary Carmody said the habit was discussed at breakfast the next morning at the Inn. Wendell must have overheard."

Josh nodded. "He did. He admitted that in his confession. He knew Godwink had died in prison and thought if the habit was there, maybe the rest of the money was too."

Terry threw in, "But we complicated things. With the haunted house thing going on, it would be difficult to search for it."

"Yes," Mansell said. And remember the plan was to burn it after Halloween. So when he overheard Barbara making plans to meet Art Carnel there—sorry, Camille—he saw it as an opportunity to get into the house and search. He thought there would be some way of sneaking in and avoiding them."

"So Art had nothing to do with any of it?" Max asked.

"According to Art, he arrived at the house and unlocked it, but left because he got a call from a potential client. Wendell's story jives with that—he got there, the house was unlocked, and no one was there."

Melody shook her head. "I feel so sorry for Barbara."

"She had terrible luck," Mansell said. "Wendell had started searching outside when Barbara showed up. She asked him what he was doing—an innocent question for someone not guilty. Wendell said he panicked—he knew she could identify him from the Inn—and strangled her. Then he got the idea to stage her in place of the manikin. He knew that would cause the house to close early and he hoped he would have more time to search. And that's the story."

147

"Amazing," Camille said. "Half of the stolen money was in the bank the whole time. And the missing manikin was in the dining room the whole time." She shook her head. "Well, I've learned something too. I'm done with Art. And I am so glad I never invested with him. This makes the break much cleaner."

"Good," Mansell said. "Art isn't off the hook. He's got a lot of explaining to do about what he did with Barbara's money, and while we're at it, we'll check out his other clients, too."

"What about the haunted house?" Max asked. "There's still over a week until Halloween. It's a shame to lose out after all of your work."

Camille clapped her hands with delight. "I almost forgot! I got a call from Fred Polk right before I left to come out here. He has an old empty house on the south edge of town that we can use."

Terry nodded. "Some people who would resent reopening the Kell house as being disrespectful to the woman who died. And it is."

Camille turned to him. "What do you think, Terry? Could we move everything this weekend and be ready to reopen Sunday night?"

Terry nodded. "If we get a small but efficient crew, I don't see why not. We wouldn't have to build anything — just move it all and hook it back up."

Lil said, "I won't be much help.

Max grinned. You can say that again."

Lil wrinkled her nose at her sister. "I'll do what we can, and then we'll be taking off on Sunday. As the saying goes, I think that's where we came in."

"We haven't figured out how you're going to get in that car yet," Terry said. "You have to share with Rosie."

"Maybe I'll just drive." Lil smiled.

THANK YOU...

For taking your time to share Max and Lil's adventures. Just as the sound of a tree falling in the forest depends on hearers, a book only matters if it has readers. Please consider sharing your thoughts with other readers in a review on Amazon and/or Goodreads. Or email me at karen.musser.nortman@gmail.com.

My website at http://www.karenmussernortman.com provides updates on my books, my blog, and photos of our for-real camping trips. Sign up on my website for my email list and get a free download of *Bats and Bones*.

To my Beta readers, Ginge, Elaine, and Marcia, thank you for all of the great catches and suggestions. And to all of my readers, especially my advance reader team, words are not enough.

The inspiration for the Mystery Sisters was memories of my Great Aunt Mary, who taught phys ed in Missouri until she was in her seventies. She owned a Studebaker and during the summer would drive up to southern Minnesota, pick up my grandmother, and off they'd go to California or Connecticut or some other exotic place (in my teenaged mind). My cousin says they argued constantly, but they made trip after trip. I stole the names of the sisters (but not the personalities) from three of my youngest aunts--the ones who were between my and my parents generation. They were the 'cool' aunts—young and hip. And they were a great example to us all.

OTHER BOOKS BY THE AUTHOR

THE MYSTERY SISTERS

Reunion and Revenge: Maxine Berra and Lillian Garrett, sisters in their seventies, travel together to visit friends and relatives in Max's 1950 red Studebaker with her Irish Setter, Rosie. Does that mean they are amicable companions? Not at all. But when, during a family reunion, the murder of a family friend throws suspicion on their shiftless younger brother, they put their heads together to try to save him.

THE AWARD-WINNING FRANNIE SHOEMAKER CAMPGROUND MYSTERIES:

Bats and Bones: (An IndieBRAG Medallion honoree) Frannie and Larry Shoemaker are retirees who enjoy weekend camping with their friends in state parks. They anticipate the usual hiking, campfires, good food, and interesting side trips among the bluffs of beautiful Bat Cave State Park for the long Fourth of July weekend — until a dead body turns up. Frannie's persistence and curiosity helps authorities sort through the possible suspects and motives, but almost ends her new sleuth career — and her life — for good.

The Blue Coyote: (An IndieBRAG Medallion honoree and a 2013 Chanticleer CLUE finalist) Frannie and Larry Shoemaker love taking their grandchildren, Sabet and Joe, camping with them. But at Bluffs State Park, Frannie finds herself worrying more than usual about their safety, and when another young girl disappears from the campground in broad daylight, her fears increase. The fun of a bike ride, a flea market, marshmallow guns, and a storyteller are quickly overshadowed. Accusations against Larry and her add to the cloud over their heads.

Peete and Repeat: (An IndieBRAG Medallion honoree, 2013 Chanticleer CLUE finalist, and 2014 Chanticleer Mystery and Mayhem finalist) A biking and camping trip to southeastern Minnesota turns into double trouble for Frannie Shoemaker and her friends as she deals with a canoeing mishap and a couple of bodies. Frannie tries to stay out of it--really--but what can she do?

The Lady of the Lake: (An IndieBRAG Medallion honoree, 2014 Chanticleer CLUE finalist) A trip down memory lane is fine if you don't stumble on a body. Frannie Shoemaker and her friends camp at Old Dam Trail State Park near one of Donna Nowak's childhood homes. But the present intrudes when a body surfaces. Donna becomes the focus of the investigation and Frannie wonders if the police shouldn't be looking closer at the victim's many enemies. A traveling goddess worshipper, a mystery writer and the Sisters on the Fly add color to the campground.

To Cache a Killer: Geocaching isn't supposed to be about finding dead bodies. But when retiree, Frannie

Shoemaker go camping, standard definitions don't apply. A weekend in a beautiful state park in Iowa buzzes with fund-raising events, a search for Ninja turtles, a bevy of suspects, and lots of great food. But are the campers in the wrong place at the wrong time once too often?

The Space Invader: A cozy/thriller mystery! The starry skies over New Mexico, the "Land of Enchantment," may hold secrets of their own. The Shoemakers and the Ferraros, on an extended camping trip, find themselves picking up a souvenir they don't want and taking side trips they didn't plan on.

Real Actors, Not People: Frannie Shoemaker and her friends go camping to get away from the real world. So they are surprised and dismayed to find their wilderness campground the production site of a new 'reality' show-- Celebrity Campout. Reality intrudes on their week in the form of accidents, nature, and even murder. They handle the situation with their usual humor, compassion, and mystery solving, because...camping can be murder.

We are NOT Buying a Camper! A prequel to the Frannie Shoemaker Campground Mysteries. Frannie and Larry Shoemaker have busy jobs, two teenagers, and plenty of other demands on their time and sanity. Larry's sister and brother-in-law pester them to try camping for relaxation-- time to sit back, enjoy nature, and catch up on naps. Join Frannie as "RV there yet?" becomes "RV crazy?" and she learns that going back to nature doesn't necessarily mean a simpler life.

A Campy Christmas: A Holiday novella. The Shoemakers and Ferraros plan to spend Christmas in Texas and then take a camping trip through the Southwest. But those plans are stopped cold when they hit a rogue ice storm in Missouri and they end up snowbound in a campground. And that's just the beginning. Includes recipes and winter camping tips.

Happy Camper Tips and Recipes: All of the tips and recipes from the first four Frannie Shoemaker books in one convenient paperback or Kindle version that you can keep in your camping supplies.

THE TIME TRAVEL TRAILER SERIES

The Time Travel Trailer: (An IndieBRAG Medallion honoree, 2015 Chanticleer Paranormal First-in-Category winner) A 1937 vintage camper trailer half hidden in weeds catches Lynne McBriar's eye when she is visiting an elderly friend Ben. Ben eagerly sells it to her and she just as eagerly embarks on a restoration. But after each remodel, sleeping in the trailer lands Lynne and her daughter Dinah in a previous decade—exciting, yet frightening. Glimpses of their home town and ancestors fifty or sixty years earlier is exciting and also offers some clues to the mystery of Ben's lost love. But when Dinah makes a trip on her own, separating herself from her mother by decades, Lynne has never known such fear. It is a trip that may upset the future if Lynne and her estranged husband can't team up to bring their daughter back.

Trailer on the Fly: How many of us have wished at some time or other we could go back in time and change an action or a decision or just take back something that was said? But it is what it is. There is no rewind, reboot, delete key or any other trick to change the past, right?

Lynne McBriar can. She bought a 1937 camper that turned out to be a time portal. And when she meets a young woman who suffers from serious depression over the loss of a close friend ten years earlier, she has the power to do something about it. And there is no reason not to use that power. Right?

Trailer, Get Your Kicks!: Lynne McBriar swore her vintage trailer would stay in a museum where it would be safe from further time travel. But when a museum in Texas wants to borrow it, she determines that she must deliver it herself. Her husband Kurt convinces her to take it along Route 66 for research he is doing. What starts out as a family vacation soon turns deadly, and ends with a romance unworn by time. Travel can be dangerous any time, but when your trip involves the Time Travel Trailer, who knows where (or when) you will end up?

ABOUT THE AUTHOR

Karen Musser Nortman is the author of the Frannie Shoemaker Campground cozy mystery series, including several BRAGMedallion honorees. After previous incarnations as a secondary social studies teacher (22 years) and a test developer (18 years), she returned to her childhood dream of writing a novel. The Frannie Shoemaker Campground Mysteries came out of numerous 'round the campfire' discussions, making up answers to questions raised by the peephole glimpses one gets into the lives of fellow campers. Where did those people disappear to for the last two days? What kinds of bones are in this fire pit? Why is that woman wearing heels to the shower house?

Karen and her husband Butch originally tent camped when their children were young and switched to a travel trailer when sleeping on the ground lost its romantic adventure. They take frequent weekend jaunts with friends to parks in Iowa and surrounding states, plus occasional longer trips. Entertainment on these trips has ranged from geocaching and hiking/biking to barbecue contests, balloon fests, and buck skinners' rendezvous.

Sign up for Karen's email list at www.karenmussernortman.com and receive a free ereader download of *Bats and Bones.*

25408220R00100

Made in the USA
Lexington, KY
19 December 2018